"I Came To Ask You To Come Back Home And Practice Medicine,"

Hayley said.

"Let me get this straight. You want a high-priced heart surgeon to come back to the place that ran him out of town to play Family Practitioner to the few remaining inhabitants?"

"We're desperate."

"I wouldn't go back if they offered me the Nobel Prize."

"I'm afraid we can't do that, but—"

"But what? You'll give me a chance to live on the right side of the tracks for a change? Or respect... admiration? No, thanks. I prefer the life I have and the patients who pay me lots of cold, hard cash for my services."

She winced. Was that really why he'd become a doctor? After his dirt-poor, poverty-stricken childhood, she couldn't blame him for wanting security.

"Of course you wouldn't understand that," he continued. "Being a Bancroft, you've always had everything you ever wanted."

Everything except for you, she thought.

Dear Reader,

In keeping with the celebration of Silhouette's 20th anniversary in 2000, what better way to enjoy the new century's first Valentine's Day than to read six passionate, powerful, provocative love stories from Silhouette Desire!

Beloved author Dixie Browning returns to Desire's MAN OF THE MONTH promotion with *A Bride for Jackson Powers,* also the launch title for the series THE PASSIONATE POWERS. Enjoy this gem about a single dad who becomes stranded with a beautiful widow who's his exact opposite.

Get ready to be seduced when Alexandra Sellers offers you another sheikh hero from her SONS OF THE DESERT miniseries with *Sheikh's Temptation.* Maureen Child's popular series BACHELOR BATTALION continues with *The Daddy Salute*—a marine turns helpless when he must take care of his baby, and he asks the heroine for help.

Kate Little brings you a keeper with *Husband for Keeps,* in which the heroine needs an in-name-only husband in order to hold on to her ranch. A fabulously sexy doctor returns to the woman he could never forget in *The Magnificent M.D.* by Carol Grace. And exciting newcomer Sheri WhiteFeather offers another irresistible Native American hero in *Jesse Hawk: Brave Father.*

We hope you will indulge yourself this Valentine's Day with all six of these passionate romances, only from Silhouette Desire!

Enjoy!

Joan Marlow Golan

Joan Marlow Golan
Senior Editor, Silhouette Desire

Please address questions and book requests to:
Silhouette Reader Service
U.S.: 3010 Walden Ave., P.O. Box 1325, Buffalo, NY 14269
Canadian: P.O. Box 609, Fort Erie, Ont. L2A 5X3

The Magnificent M.D.

CAROL GRACE

Published by Silhouette Books
America's Publisher of Contemporary Romance

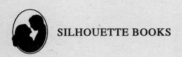 **SILHOUETTE BOOKS**

ISBN 0-373-76277-1

THE MAGNIFICENT M.D.

Printed in U.S.A.

Books by Carol Grace

Silhouette Desire

Wife for a Night #1118
The Heiress Inherits a Cowboy #1145
Expecting... #1205
The Magnificent M.D. #1277

Silhouette Romance

Make Room for Nanny #690
A Taste of Heaven #751
Home Is Where the Heart Is #882
Mail-Order Male #955
The Lady Wore Spurs #1010
*Lonely Millionaire #1057
*Almost a Husband #1105
*Almost Married #1142
The Rancher and the Lost Bride #1153
†Granted: Big Sky Groom #1277
†Granted: Wild West Bride #1303
†Granted: A Family for Baby #1345
Married to the Sheik #1391

*Miramar Inn
†Best-Kept Wishes

CAROL GRACE

has always been interested in travel and living abroad.
She spent her junior year in college in France and toured
the world working on the hospital ship *Hope*. She and
her husband spent the first year and a half of their marriage in Iran, where they both taught English. Then, with
their toddler daughter, they lived in Algeria for two
years.

Carol says that writing is another way of making her life
exciting. Her office is her mountaintop home, which
overlooks the Pacific Ocean and which she shares with
her inventor husband, their daughter, who just graduated
college, and their teenage son.

IT'S OUR 20th ANNIVERSARY!
We'll be celebrating all year, continuing with these fabulous titles, on sale in February 2000.

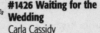

One

Hayley Bancroft walked into the waiting room of the medical office at 450 Sutter Street, San Francisco, a little after five o'clock. The faint smell of medicinal alcohol brought back memories of her grandfather's office: his waiting room packed with mothers and babies waiting for checkups, old folks with arthritis and an occasional kid with a cast on his leg just begging to be autographed. She thought of him, the essence of the small-town doctor, peering through his bifocals as he soothingly reassured his patients. He knew everybody in town, cared about them, was never too tired to make house calls. She missed him so intensely she had to blink back a tear as the memories came rushing back. The receptionist cleared her throat and turned off her computer which nudged Hayley out of her reverie.

"The doctor isn't seeing any new patients," she told Hayley brusquely.

Hayley took a deep breath. "I'm not a new patient. I'm an old...an old friend."

"He isn't seeing any old friends, either." The woman checked her watch, reached under her desk for her purse and stood, eyeing Hayley coolly. "He isn't seeing anyone."

The sound of deep male voices rumbled from behind a heavy mahogany door with Samuel J. Prentice M.D. printed on it in gold letters. And underneath the name, the word Cardiology. Oh, Lord, she was hoping Sam was a family practitioner, not a specialist. But beggars couldn't be choosers. And Hayley was prepared to beg, if necessary. Anything to convince him to come back to New Hope. If he didn't...she didn't know what to do next. She'd tried everything and everyone else. The town was counting on her.

She met the woman's steely gaze head-on. So he was there. And he *was* seeing *someone*. Since she hadn't come a thousand miles to be turned back by some starchy guardian of the shrine of Dr. Sam Prentice, she took a seat in a large faux-leather chair under a tasteful still-life painting and curled her fingers around the edge of the seat cushion.

"I'll wait," she said. After all, what could Nurse Ratchet do, throw her out forcibly?

For a long moment the receptionist stood at the door, perhaps contemplating just that—tossing her out on her ear. Hayley met her gaze and didn't waver. She had nothing to lose and everything to gain. Finally the woman shrugged her narrow shoulders, shoved her arms into the sleeves of her sweater and left.

The voices behind the closed door got louder. Hayley couldn't resist. Any scrap of information could help her cause. After a brief moment's hesitation she walked softly across the thick carpet and pressed her ear against the door.

"Dammit to hell, Al, I'm not leaving the hospital," Sam shouted. "I've got a full surgery schedule up through September and a waiting list of electives. As long as I've got patients I'm going to stay here and operate on them. Is that clear?"

Hayley hadn't heard him speak for some seventeen years, since he'd left New Hope, but the sound of his voice reverberated through her like a bell, sending shock waves through her body. He sounded just as bullheaded, just as stubborn as ever. It was enough to send an ordinary person scrambling for cover. What made her think she could talk him into coming back home? Unless she used her ultimate weapon. She'd given her word she would never use it, never tell him. But if her grandfather knew what was at stake, wouldn't he have given her the go-ahead? Wouldn't he have agreed that his office needed to be filled, that the people in her town wanted, needed, deserved a doctor?

"Look, Sam, I'm not asking you to retire. I'm asking you to take a break, a year or at least six months off. How bad can that be?" Al asked.

"How bad? I'll tell you how bad. Surgery is what I do. It's what I am. Ever since medical school I've been working eighteen-hour days. I intend to continue."

"Until when? Until you make a serious mistake? When will you realize you're burned out, that you're overscheduled and overworked and you desperately need to take some time off?"

"Are you referring to the patient I lost over the weekend, because if you are, I did everything humanly possible—"

"I know you did. When I ask you to take time off I'm not only thinking about your patients. I'm thinking about you. I'm thinking about your health—your mental health. Look at you, you're tense, you're irritable, you're on the verge of cracking. I care about you, Sam. I care about your future. Which I hope will be long and productive. I saw you Sunday after you broke the news to your patient's family.''

''You saw me, okay, so I lost it. I failed and I felt bad about it. I don't like to fail. I don't like to lose a patient. It's not that unusual to have a reaction.''

''It's unusual to take it out on the nurses. It's unusual to punch a hole in the door of the supply room.''

Sam muttered something, but Hayley couldn't make it out.

''You tell me,'' Al continued. ''Tell me what you'd say if I was your patient. If I had your symptoms. You know what they are. Short temper. Chip on shoulder. Runaway ambition and drive. You'd tell me to take a break. To bug off for six months to a year. To do something different. Something besides surgery. Anything.''

''No. The answer is no,'' Sam said brusquely. ''I'm not taking a break. I'm not going anywhere.''

''That was not a request Sam,'' Al said. ''That was an order. You're a fine surgeon. We need you here. But not in your present condition. Either you take a leave or I'll fire you. I'm doing this for your own good. I want you to come back with a fresh outlook and a new attitude. You're young, you've got years ahead of you. You've been working eighty-hour weeks for what…ten, fifteen years? Take the damn six months off.''

There was a long silence. Hayley could picture Sam pacing back and forth, jaw clenched, seething. Then he finally spoke.

''Let's say I agree to take a break. What am I supposed to do for six months?''

''I don't know. Get a hobby. Take a cruise. Play golf.

Catch up on your reading in obscure medical journals. Find a woman who'll put up with you and get married.''

"That's your solution to everything. Find a woman. I've tried it...it doesn't work."

Hayley recognized the cynicism in his voice. He hadn't changed. At least his attitude hadn't. She wondered what he looked like after so many years. She pictured the dark curly hair that he'd worn long and wild. The cleft in his chin, the broken nose from a fight in high school, the high cheekbones and the black eyes with the insolent expression.

"Then choose your own poison. Do something different. Anything. Cut out the long workdays. Get away from here. Get out of town. How many ways can I say it?"

Hayley leaned against the door, gripping the doorknob for support. So he wasn't married. Not that it mattered. Not to her. What would he do now? Would he take his boss's advice? The old Sam didn't do well with authority figures. Didn't like taking orders. The old Sam sounded very much like the new Sam as a matter of fact. Stubborn, hardheaded and proud. She was hoping he'd changed, mellowed into a genial family practitioner. She should have known better.

"I hear you, Al. Now get out. I've got some thinking to do," Sam said.

"I'll expect your request for medical leave tomorrow," Al said.

"Al..."

"All right, I'm going," Al said.

Before she could retreat, the man opened the door, and Hayley fell forward and stumbled into the office.

There was a long moment of silence. It was hard to tell who was more surprised. Sam, who was staring at her as if she'd fallen out of the sky, his boss, who was blinking owlishly behind horn-rims, or Hayley herself. This wasn't how she'd planned to meet Sam. She needed all the poise and all the ammunition she could get. To be caught eavesdropping put her at a disadvantage to say the least.

When she'd finally caught her breath and regained her balance, everyone spoke at once.

"What in the hell…"

"Who are you?"

"I—I'm sorry, I…"

"One of your patients, Sam?" Al asked.

Sam frowned as if he was trying to decide if she was indeed one of his patients or one of those women he'd tried it with and it hadn't worked out or the wife of a colleague or…

"Hayley Bancroft," she said, unable to stand the silence any longer. "From New Hope."

Sam's eyes narrowed. He leaned back against his desk and surveyed her from the top of her casually tousled blond hair down the simple black suit she'd chosen after trying on everything else in her closet, to the low-heeled shoes she'd been walking around town in trying to get up enough nerve to come in to his office.

"Hayley Bancroft," Sam repeated, still staring. "What in the hell are you doing here?"

"It's a long story," she said.

"Sounds interesting," Al said. "I wish I could stay and hear it, but I'm out of here. Don't forget what I said." He shot a pointed look at Sam, gave Hayley an appreciative glance and closed the door behind him.

She'd practiced over and over what she would say, but now that she was here her mind went blank. She'd thought, she'd hoped, that Sam might have changed in the past seventeen years. She couldn't have imagined he'd be even more good-looking as a mature, confident physician than he ever was as a bad boy. Or that he might be more dangerous to her well-being than the day he'd left New Hope for good. But he was.

"It's good to see you, Sam. It's been a long time," she said. There, it wasn't very original, but it was an opening. And she'd even kept her voice steady.

"Has it?" There it was, that damn-your-eyes tone of his. The tone that said, the hell with you, the hell with New Hope and everyone in it. Except for her grandfather. Sam and Grandpa had had a special relationship, until the end. But at the end it wasn't enough to save Sam. Eventually Sam had saved himself. With a little help.

"What brings you down here, Hayley?" he asked, as if she were only an old acquaintance he barely remembered. Maybe she was. Maybe she'd magnified what was once just a one-sided teenage crush on the town bad boy into the lost love of her life. She envied his attitude. If only she could be so cool, calm and collected, so downright *indifferent* about seeing him again. Instead her heart was pounding, and she was fighting off the urge to run out of there and never come back. If it weren't for the whole town counting on her...if it weren't for the legacy her grandfather had left—

"Can I sit down?" Her knees were so weak that if she didn't sit fast, she'd fall down.

He shrugged, and she gratefully sank into a real leather chair while he remained standing, arms crossed over his waist.

"I came to ask a favor," she said.

"What do you need? A bypass, angioplasty, a pacemaker?" His bold gaze traveled over her body causing an outbreak of goose bumps all over her skin.

"No, thanks, not yet," she said.

"I didn't think so. You look as if you're in pretty good

shape," he said with an appreciative half smile. "For your age."

"Thank you," she said. "So do you." That was the understatement of the year. The hair had been tamed, the boyish features had hardened, solidified into the face of a ruggedly handsome man. A man who obviously still took chances, still did things his own way and who'd overcome a mountain of obstacles to get what and where he wanted. A man who once had nothing, but now seemed to have everything except for a calm, steady temperament. She couldn't blame him for his attitude toward her. Of course he wasn't glad to see her. He remembered only what he thought she'd done to him. She and her grandfather.

"Get to the point, Hayley. You didn't come all this way so we could exchange compliments."

How brusque he was. How cold and uncaring. She should have known. She should have expected it. She took a deep breath. It was now or never. "No. I came to ask you to come back and practice medicine in New Hope."

"What?" His stunned tone indicated that she'd finally captured his wholehearted attention.

"My grandfather died a year ago," she blurted out. "We're looking for a doctor to take his place."

"Let me get this straight. You want a high-priced heart surgeon to come back to the place that ran him out of town and play family practitioner to the few remaining inhabitants?"

"I didn't know you were a high-priced surgeon. Not until a half hour ago. I was hoping you'd be a GP like Grandpa. Not that anyone could fill his shoes, but if you're worried that people won't accept you—"

"I don't give a damn if the people of New Hope accept me or not. I wouldn't go back there if they offered me the Nobel Prize."

"I'm afraid we can't do that, but—"

"But what? You'll give me your grandfather's old office on Main Street where the grateful patients leave a bushel of apples on the front steps when they can't pay? Or maybe a membership in the so-called country club? A chance to live on the right side of the tracks for a change? Or respect...admiration? No, thanks. I prefer the life I have. Challenging, cutting-edge procedures. Brilliant colleagues. And patients who pay for my services. Cold, hard cash."

She winced at his blunt admission. She could understand his needing a challenge and stimulating company. His brain always ran twice as fast as anyone else's. But what about his need for money? Was that really why he'd become a doctor? Knowing his background, she really couldn't blame him for wanting security. After a dirt-poor, poverty-stricken childhood, he was then abandoned by his parents. Why shouldn't he want a roof over his head and the knowledge he could buy whatever he wanted? The things most people took for granted had been missing from his childhood. Why shouldn't he want a different kind of life than the one he'd known in New Hope? She had. She'd left town to find it. But she'd made a decision to come back. She had to convince him to come back too.

"You wouldn't understand that," he continued. "Being a Bancroft. You've always had everything you ever wanted."

Everything. Except him, she thought. Once she'd wanted him so badly she thought she'd die from longing. Everything except a stable income. And even more important, everything except the love of a good man and a child of her own. But she'd come to terms with her life. Other women her age had a husband and children and security. But though she'd given up on the husband and children part, she was working on financial security by running a successful inn. Besides, she had a whole town, a town that needed her. She couldn't let them down.

"Everything?" she repeated softly. "Not really. Even the money is gone now."

"What? The Bancrofts without money? That's like a train without tracks. A circus without the big top. What happened?"

She sighed and looked at her watch.

"I see. It's a long story. Maybe some other time." He shifted his gaze to the door so pointedly she'd have to be blind not to realize how much he wanted her gone.

But he was not getting rid of her that easily. She stood and put her hand on his arm before he could take action. "Sam, please. I know how you feel about my family."

"And you," he said, removing her hand from his arm as if she had a communicable disease.

"And me, yes, I know. But just give me a chance to explain. Can I buy you a cup of coffee?"

"Can you afford it?" he asked, his voice laced with irony.

"Yes, I can afford it. If you have the time."

"Time? I have nothing but time," he said bitterly. "I have six months of time."

The coffee shop was on the first floor, and Sam was glad to see it was empty except for a stranger drinking a smoothie at the juice bar. Sam didn't want to speak to anyone. He especially didn't want to speak to Hayley. But as much as he wanted to turn his back on her, he couldn't. Not quite yet. Not when the memories were threatening to overwhelm him and make him feel young and poor and vulnerable again. Not until he'd gotten her out of his system again. The last time it took about ten years. This time it shouldn't take more than thirty minutes.

He certainly didn't want to have to answer any questions from colleagues who might be taking a break in the coffee shop—like what happened last week in surgery and who's the beautiful blonde you're with? And she was beautiful. And black set off her honey-blond hair. Maybe it was true that the Bancroft money was gone, but in a suit that fit her as if it was made for her, made to hug her curves and show off her long legs, she sure looked like someone who'd held onto her charge card at Nordstroms.

No question, the girl he'd known in another lifetime had turned into a stylish, sophisticated woman. And what a woman. A confident, self-assured woman with a glint of determination in her blue eyes and a firm grip on his arm. Coupled with her soft-as-cashmere voice she was damned-near irresistible. But not so irresistible that he was going to give her more than a half hour of his time. She didn't deserve it.

"Tell me," he said, as he slid into the booth opposite her. "How long were you leaning against the door eavesdropping?"

A flush spread over her face. So she hadn't completely changed after all. She wasn't quite as self-assured as she looked. He remembered the first time he'd spoken to her, freshman year in high school. She looked so beautiful, so rich, so untouchable, and he felt so poor and so disreputable. He almost walked right by her, with the usual chip on his shoulder, eyes forward, a practiced cynical sneer on his face. If she hadn't been having trouble getting her locker open, he would have.

But she was standing there, helplessly tugging at the combination lock. The bell was ringing and everyone else was rushing by, hurrying to get to class on time. Not him. He wasn't in a hurry to get anywhere. It wasn't cool. And what was the point? School was stupid, anyway.

"Something wrong?" he'd asked.

She'd glanced over her shoulder and nodded. Her face was flushed and she was chewing on her lower lip in frustration.

He'd grabbed the lock out of her hand, asked her for the combination and with a few twirls and a quick jerk, he'd opened it for her.

"How did you do that?" she'd asked, looking at him with those incredible blue eyes as if he was a superhero.

"No big deal," he'd said. And it hadn't been.

Then why would her words and the way she looked that day in her blue sweater and short, pleated cheerleader skirt be forever engraved in his memory? Why couldn't he have left it at that? A brief encounter between high school freshmen who couldn't have been more different. But no, he had to see her again after class, talk to her in the parking lot and get involved with her. Why? Because she made him feel special, like he was worth something. When everyone else told him otherwise.

She was like a drug, he realized later, one of those pain killers he prescribed routinely for his post-op patients. In the same way that the pills gave relief to his patients, she'd helped ease the pain in his life. And like those pills she was addictive. Even now, seeing her again, he felt the way he had that day, inexplicably drawn to her, unable to look away, unable to stay away.

He thought he'd broken the addiction. He hadn't thought of her for years. Not much, anyway. It was too painful, and though he was many things, he was not a masochist. But here she was back in his life. Showing him that she still had the power to make his pulse rate speed up as if he'd just run the Bay to Breakers Race. Still had the power to make him feel as though he was special and that he could do anything. Why? Not because she'd missed him over the years. Not because he meant anything to her then or now. Because she wanted a favor. She wanted him to come back to the town that hated him. And for what? To check a few sore throats, prescribe some ulcer medicine and set a broken arm or two.

He'd done a six-month rotation in general practice a long time ago and soon realized it was not for him. He didn't have the patience to deal with minor problems and nonspecific complaints. No, he was a surgeon, on the cutting edge, so to speak, of the latest procedures, giving lectures at the medical school, writing articles or presenting papers at a conference.

She stirred her coffee before she answered his question. "I wasn't out there very long. I couldn't hear much of anything."

"But you tried."

"Yes," she admitted with a sheepish smile. "I tried. We're desperate."

"We?"

"The town council. The search committee. The mayor. The school board. The PTA. Everyone who lives in New Hope. We've done everything. Advertised in medical schools, interviewed retirees, promised free housing. But doctors these days want more than that. They want to live in big cities. We tried to persuade them that small towns have their own charms. We can offer clean air and beautiful beaches and friendly, grateful people. But they want more than that. They want to make a lot of money," Hayley said, "and that's one thing we haven't got."

"After all those years of school, of going without sleep or money or good times, can you blame them?" Sam asked.

"No, no, of course not. But we need somebody so desperately. It's a three-hour drive to Portland and the nearest doctor,'' Hayley said.

"Over a winding road," he noted.

"You remember," she said.

"I can't forget," he said flatly.

"In just this last year, since Grandpa died, we've had three serious emergencies. A baby was born with complications. Henry Mills had a stroke and Mrs. Gompers died of a heart attack. If we'd had a doctor in town…"

"But you didn't," he said, setting his cup down on the table with an air of finality. "I hope you find one, but I'm not your man."

"I can understand your reluctance to come back," she said, "but—"

"Reluctance is putting it mildly," he said. "Shall I go over the reasons?"

"I think I can guess. You don't want to return to small-town life."

"That's a good start. Go on."

"You're a surgeon and you feel general practice is beneath you."

"Correction. I'm a surgeon and I don't do general practice. I haven't done it since I was an intern, and then I only did it for six months. Let me be frank. I wasn't cut out for it. I can't deal with the nonspecific complaints, the colds, the flu and the heartburn. I take patients who would die without my help, and I do valve replacements and heart transplants, and I give them their lives back. Am I making myself clear?"

"Yes, of course. But you could do it for a while. Treat the sore throats and the minor complaints. You wouldn't even have to brush up."

"I'm not supposed to work for six months. And that's that."

"That's not what he said," she said. "He said 'cut out the long workdays and get out of town.'"

"So you *were* listening," he said.

"I couldn't help it. You were talking so loudly I'm surprised the whole building didn't hear your conversation," she said.

"The whole building didn't have their ears pressed against the door," he said.

"You wouldn't have to work that hard, really, if that's what you're worried about," she continued before he could come up with another excuse. "I've got someone to help you do the bookkeeping, wrap bandages, hold the strobe lights and refill the tongue depressors, order supplies and hand you the instruments."

"Now who would that be?" he asked.

"That would be Mattie Whitlock," Hayley said. "Grandpa's old nurse. She's had years of experience. And she's ready and willing to help out."

"She's still there? She must be about ninety-five by now."

"Seventy-three. She's slowed down somewhat, but she's still got the touch."

"Yeah, I remember her touch," Sam said grimly. "And the way she wielded a needle. I was more scared of her than anyone in town, including the police." He shook his head, already regretting that he'd admitted being scared of anything. He didn't want to admit it, he didn't want to remember it. The pain and the shame he'd felt in those days still lingered beneath the surface. After all these years. Until Hayley had walked into his office, he hadn't realized how deep it went. He wished she'd stayed where she was and left him alone. "No," he said. "I'm not coming back and that's final."

"What are you going to do? Take up golf? Get a hobby?

Read medical journals or find a woman to marry?'' The skepticism in her voice was unmistakable.

''Any one of those ideas is sounding better by the minute,'' he said.

''I'm not asking you to make a permanent commitment,'' she said. ''Just a year, or even six months. Your patients will still be here when you return. All I'm asking is that you come back until we find a permanent doctor. It'll be like a vacation. You can go deep-sea fishing. Dig for clams. Take Wednesday afternoons off to play golf at the club. Maybe even find a woman to marry. Small-town women may not be as glamorous as the ones you're used to but they may not be as superficial, either.''

He let his gaze roam over her fashionably tousled, Meg Ryan-style blond hair, her suit jacket and the silk blouse under it. Deliberately avoiding his eyes, she tore open a packet of sugar and poured it into what remained of her coffee.

''Are you including yourself?'' he asked with a gleam in his eye. ''If you are, I might be tempted.''

''No, of course not,'' she said indignantly.

''Sure? Because you fit the description—small-town girl, not superficial…''

''I told you, I'm not,'' she said, bright spots of color in her cheeks. ''I'm not available.''

''Why not? Is there a man in your life?''

''There's a town in my life. A town that needs a doctor. Now can we get back to the subject at hand?''

''Why not. Tell me, who would I play golf with?'' he asked. He'd forgotten how it felt to tease her, to flirt with her, catch her off-guard and watch her blush. Sitting across from her in a vinyl-covered booth reminded him of Scotty's Drug Store, the New Hope teen hangout, where instead of sitting across from her, he used to walk by,

hands in his pocket, collar of his flannel shirt up against
the wind, and look in the window. There she would be
with her high school friends, the cream of New Hope society, laughing and talking and eating French fries. Everyone she hung out with was like her—respectable, well
dressed, beautiful and well off—everything he wasn't.
Sometimes he'd catch her eye. She would stop and stare
out the window at him. He'd shrug nonchalantly and walk
away to show he hadn't been looking at her at all and he
didn't care that he wasn't part of the crowd. Everything
had changed since then, and yet nothing had really
changed at all.

"Me, I'd play with you," she said.

"You play golf?" he asked. He shouldn't be surprised.
Golf was a classy sport, an expensive sport, the kind
played at the country club by people like the Bancrofts
and their crowd...a crowd that didn't appeal to him then
or now. But golf did. And he'd never had time to work on
his game.

"I'm probably a little rusty."

"Is that all?" he asked.

"No, of course not. Besides the golf course at the country club there's much more. There's a bookstore now and
an art gallery, even a bed and breakfast, but what we really
need is a—"

"A bed and breakfast? What was wrong with the old
boarding house?"

"Oh, it's still there. Maudie has a steady clientele who
rent by the week, but—"

"But that's not good enough for the new, improved
town. They had to have a B&B. So what else can I look
forward to besides golf, when I'm giving up my life for
six months?" he asked. He was curious to see just how
far she would go to get him back.

"What more do you want from me, Sam, besides wholesome, outdoor activities? Apologies, explanations?" She looked up at him with those incredible aquamarine eyes that could always see deep down inside him. He couldn't let her do that. Not now. Not ever again. He'd trusted her once too often, and he'd paid the price. He met her gaze with a practiced, noncommittal, cool look that gave away nothing. He hoped.

"Apologies and explanations would be a start, yes. But I'm not going back to New Hope," he said, setting his cup down with a loud bang. "Ever. Not for you. Not for anyone. Is that clear?"

"Yes," she murmured, but her eyes said no, it wasn't. Apparently it wasn't clear and she wasn't finished with him yet. Lord, she was maddening. Just as determined as she'd been at eighteen. Maybe more so. But he wasn't eighteen anymore. He'd built up a fortress of defenses since then. He'd carefully roped off his childhood from questions and inquiries. Now he was face-to-face with someone who knew all about him. The sooner he got rid of her, the better.

She reached across the table and gently ran her fingers across his palm. It was just a casual gesture, but coming from her it was incredibly sensual. His gaze locked on hers for a long moment, and his heart thudded. His hand throbbed, the hand he'd used to take out his frustrations on a door last Sunday. He yanked it away and broke eye contact.

He had to get up and leave, to get out of there, to get away from her, but for some reason, he couldn't move. Not with her sitting there, looking at him expectantly, with the ceiling lights turning her blond hair to gold. Waiting for him to give in and say yes. Which he was not going to do.

"You've told me more than I want to know about New Hope, Hayley, but precious little about yourself. You haven't answered my question. Is there a man in your life? Are you married?" he asked, his voice carefully neutral, just to let her know it really didn't matter, he was only mildly curious.

"Not anymore."

He kept his face a mask of indifference, but inside he heaved a sigh of relief. He didn't know why. He didn't really care if she was married to the mayor and had five kids. It made absolutely no difference to him.

She shifted in her seat and looked over his shoulder, avoiding his gaze. "I prefer not to talk about it if you don't mind."

"You don't want to talk about your past, and I don't want to talk about my future. Maybe we ought to call it a day," he said.

"Not yet," she said, tucking one leg under the other on the vinyl bench. "I don't mind talking about my past, it's just my marriage that I'd rather forget."

"That bad?"

"That bad. What about you?"

"Doctors make lousy spouses."

"Too busy?" she asked.

"Busy, unfaithful, self-centered, arrogant. You name it. So I never married. And have no intention of doing so."

"Girlfriends?" she asked.

"When it's convenient," he said.

"For you, not them," she said with a wry smile.

"Of course," he said. "They come and go."

"Mostly go," she muttered, and gave a little shiver of disapproval. She obviously understood only too well. The description of doctors and of his lifestyle disgusted her, and he almost wished he could take it back. He didn't have to explain he was guilty of most of the above, he could tell by the look in her eyes she thought it went with the territory. He'd never been unfaithful, though, he wanted her to know that. But then he'd never been faithful, either, because there was nobody to be faithful to. Let her think the worst of him. It was better that way. He had an uncontrollable desire to reach across the table and take her hand. So he did. Just a random, casual gesture. He found that her fingers were frigid.

"You're cold," he said. "You need something hot to eat and so do I." He ordered two bowls of clam chowder before she had a chance to protest that she wasn't hungry or that she was watching her weight. Many of the women he saw professionally or socially were on strict diets and often suffered from severe cases of vanity and self-absorption. Could Hayley be any different? She could be anything. He didn't know her anymore. But God help him, he wanted to. He wanted to know where she'd been and who'd she'd been with and what she'd been doing.... He shouldn't ask, he knew he shouldn't, but he did.

"Go on," he said. "What did you do with that expensive college education your parents paid for?"

"A little of this, a little of that. Nothing very useful, I'm ashamed to say. Until I joined the Peace Corps."

"You, the prom queen, in the Peace Corps?" he asked, trying to imagine her living without running water or electricity. "What did you do?"

"I was doing what they call community development in a little village in Africa. They say it's the toughest job you'll ever have and it was. Until then I didn't realize how spoiled I was.... Don't smile, Sam, you knew I was spoiled. You told me often enough. I should have known, but I didn't. The whole experience was maddening, frustrating and demoralizing, but I learned more in those two years than I had in all the years before.''

"What, for example?'' he asked as the waitress set the bowls of steaming soup in front of them.

She crumbled a cracker slowly and deliberately into her chowder, then looked up at him. "Self-reliance, independence. But I didn't come here to talk about myself, Sam. I came—''

"I know why you came—you told me. But it's no use. I thought we agreed we'd get caught up, then you'd go back to your room at the St. Francis or wherever it is you're staying. And tomorrow you can fly home and get hold of a data base of general practitioners and find somebody else. Somebody who wants to practice in a quaint, little town on a picturesque Oregon bay...who'd appreciate the clam-digging and the fresh air. How hard can that be?''

He laced his description of New Hope with sarcasm as thick as the cream he stirred into his coffee so she wouldn't miss his meaning. To him that quaint little town had been his prison, from which he'd finally escaped. But even as he said the words he could feel the wind off the water, smell the odor of fish from the plant down at the dock, see the water crash against the breakwater as he jumped barefoot from rock to rock. No, they weren't all bad memories. Just most of them.

"I've already tried that,'' she said.

"Then try again,'' he suggested brusquely.

"Do you think I liked coming here, Sam? Do you think it was easy for me to barge into your office that way, knowing how you feel about me and my family and the town? I've tried everyone and everything. You're my last hope, Sam.''

"What part of no didn't you understand?'' he asked. "Nothing could make me go back. Nothing.'' He wanted to slam his fist on the table for emphasis, but that was probably just what she expected from a hot-headed, impulsive surgeon with a chip on his shoulder. He had to control himself, try to stay reasonable, try to get Hayley to accept his decision, go home and fade out of his life again. This time for good.

She stirred her soup thoughtfully, then folded and refolded her napkin while he watched her.

"What about your debt?" she asked at last.

"Debt? I don't have any debt. I had a scholarship to medical school. A free ride. You'll find that hard to believe. That anyone believed in me enough to invest in my future, to fund my education. But they did."

"I don't find it hard to believe. I always knew you'd be a success. I didn't know *how* successful you'd be. Not until now. Did you ever wonder who your anonymous benefactor was?" she asked, looking up at him from under her impossibly long lashes.

He set his spoon on the table and gave her a long, hard look. Their gazes locked and held as the seconds and the minutes ticked by. His jaw locked into place. His head pounded. And he knew. He knew then what he'd always wondered, what he'd always suspected, and what he'd always known deep down. That he was going back to New Hope whether he wanted to or not. Because he wasn't going to be in debt to or dependent on anyone.

"I have a feeling you're going to tell me, aren't you? Go ahead, Hayley, get it over with and make my day. That's what you came for, isn't it? That's what you've been waiting for."

Two

Before she left the next day, Hayley offered him a ride up the rugged coast in her vintage Chrysler, another legacy from her grandfather, but he declined. That was all he needed, to spend sixteen hours in a car with her...with the smell of her subtle floral perfume wafting his way, her profile always in sight, the curve of her cheek, the arch of her eyebrow. An occasional glimpse of her full breasts under her sweater.

Not that he didn't want the opportunity to hit her with some hard questions. Number one: was it fair to lay this guilt trip on him? Next: how and when and why had the scholarship come about? No doubt it had been meant to encourage him to go to med school, a poor boy, a one-time delinquent who'd barely made it through four years of undergraduate school by busing tables in the cafeteria by day and tending bar at night. But wasn't it also a way to assuage the old man's conscience, too?

There would be time to ask her. Time for her to explain, if she could, what had happened back then. There would be six months, to be exact. So he left a few days after she did, after he'd loaded his black Porsche with the tools of his trade, his notebook computer with a CD Rom and access to the latest developments in medicine from every known medical journal, updated daily, a box of medical journals, clothes and a few, very few, personal items. He didn't need much. He wasn't going to be there that long. Just long enough to pay off his debt.

He thought long and hard about the debt as he drove the coast highway. It was going to take some getting used to after years of feeling no obligation to anyone. He'd pretty much raised himself, put himself through school and now he was in practice for himself. But not out of debt. Not yet. Not for six months. It left a bitter taste in his mouth, hearing he owed her grandfather and, by extension, Hayley and the whole town. He thought he'd done it all on his own. He was proud of that.

It was a good feeling, being independent. Having no one dependent on him. After a childhood spent in poverty he was able to buy whatever he wanted, the fastest motorcycle, the most expensive sports car. Yes, he had a good life. Things were going well…except for the occasional outburst when things didn't go right. He couldn't stand losing a patient. Refused to believe it had to happen. He didn't need to take a break. He'd fully intended to go and confront Al one more time. And he would have if Hayley hadn't come back in his life…if she'd kept the secret the way her grandfather had asked her to.

He drove slowly through town, holding the memories at arm's length, trying to see it as a stranger would, instead of as the town bad boy. He noted the fragrant smell of freshly sawed Douglas fir, indicating the mill was still in operation. What did they do without a doctor in town when there were injuries? he wondered. The brick buildings on Main Street looked the same, though several shops had closed and boarded their windows. He rolled down his windows to let the salt air rush in and fill his nostrils. He'd forgotten how invigorating it could be. How stale it made all other air feel.

He couldn't bring himself to go in to Doc Bancroft's old office yet, so he drove past the office that occupied the building that had once been somebody's clapboard house. But that was way before his time. It had been the doctor's office since Sam could remember. Where the old man had practiced medicine with a firm hand. Where Sam himself had been treated for injuries more than once. And once too often. He drove slowly around the block, wondering idly where the bed and breakfast was she said she'd book him into, trying to imagine how he was going to practice general medicine in this town for one day, let alone six months.

"Stop pacing," Matilda Whitlock ordered Hayley. "And stop staring out the window. He's not coming. He never did anything he was supposed to do in his life. Why should he start now?"

"For one reason, he said he would," Hayley told the rotund nurse, veteran of several decades of service to her grandfather.

"Hah!"

"For another reason," Hayley continued, "he's changed. He's a successful surgeon. You wouldn't recognize him, Mattie."

"Want to bet? He's still a good-looking son of a gun, I suppose?"

"I guess so." Hayley bent over to straighten a stack of

recent magazines on the end table, hoping Mattie wouldn't see the flush that stained her cheeks. The woman saw far too much, remembered everything and was loyal to those she loved and unforgiving to anyone with a character flaw. Sam had had plenty. But that hadn't stopped Hayley from falling madly in love with him at first sight. Now that she was older and wiser, she no longer believed in such a phenomenon. In fact, she didn't believe she'd ever fall in love again with anyone. At first sight or second or ever.

"I'm surprised he'd even think about coming back to New Hope," the nurse said, dusting off the top of her desk. "After what happened."

"He didn't want to come, but I talked him into it. It wasn't easy, so I hope—"

"You know what I hope?" Mattie asked, cocking her head to one side. "I hope you won't go losing your head again over that boy. Getting your heart broken again."

"He's not a boy, Mattie, and I'm not an impressionable girl. I'm a grown woman, and my heart is quite safe, thank you very much. Which reminds me, did you get the results of that heart scan you had last week in Newport?"

"Don't try to change the subject," Mattie admonished.

Hayley frowned. Like so many health professionals, Mattie thought she was invincible. Either that or she was afraid to learn the results, so she hadn't taken the test. Hayley decided this wasn't the time to press the issue. Maybe Sam could persuade her... Oh, sure, Sam telling Mattie what to do? That would be the day.

"I just hope people here will forget about his past," Hayley continued, "and accept him for what he is. And I hope he likes it here. Enough to consider staying."

"Staying for good?" Mattie raised her eyebrows as if Hayley had suggested the town rise up and give Sam a standing ovation for returning home. "The idea of that boy

taking over your grandfather's practice for good, let alone
six months..." She gave a shudder of revulsion to show
her disapproval.

Hayley took a deep breath. "It's probably not going to
happen, so let's not argue about it, Mattie."

"I'm not arguing. I'm just saying I know he's not a boy
anymore, but in my mind he'll always be this town's bad
boy no matter what he's done since. And I'm not the only
one who feels that way. People don't change, Hayley."

"As I was saying," Hayley said, trying to ignore the
woman's negative attitude. "Though I know it's not likely,
I hope he'll consider staying."

"For the town's sake, of course," Mattie said dryly,
slanting a knowing look at Hayley.

"Of course for the town's sake. You know as well as I
do how much we need a doctor, how people put off getting
a checkup, postpone seeing a doctor all because it's a
three-hour drive over a winding road to a clinic. With a
doctor in town people can sleep better at night. I know I
will."

Mattie cocked her head and gave her a knowing look.
"My, my. So Sam Prentice is going to be the answer to
our prayers. Cure our insomnia. Save the town. Keep us
all healthy. What else? Bring back tourism?"

"Well..." Hayley said.

"While he's at it, how about bringing back the stores
on Main Street? I hated to see the dry-goods store close,"
Mattie admitted, "not that they carried my size, but
still..."

"I didn't say he could perform miracles. He'd be the
first to admit he hasn't ever practiced general medicine.
He's a surgeon, you know." She glanced out the window.
Where was he? What if Mattie was right and he wasn't
coming? What if he'd given in just to get rid of her and

had no intention of following through by actually coming to New Hope? She was going to feel like a fool after spreading the word they had a doctor, if only for six months.

"A surgeon? Where's he gonna do his surgery? We haven't got an operating room, last time I looked. But that's okay. Now that Sam's here everything will be fine, isn't that what you think?" Mattie demanded. "Maybe you're right. Maybe he has changed. I just don't want to see you get hurt again. That boy was trouble from the first moment I laid eyes on him and don't you forget it. You say he's changed? I've got to see that for myself. *If* he comes, that is."

"He *will* come," Hayley insisted. He had to come. She had to make it up to him. Explain what happened. The money Grandpa spent on his education was a start, but she had to do her part. Try to make him see they'd had no choice. Because she was to blame for what happened as much as her grandfather.

After another trip around the block, Sam finally parked and walked up the sidewalk past a neatly trimmed lawn to the old house with impatiens blooming brightly in the window boxes. Was that Hayley's touch? Engraved on a plaque on the door was his name. His name? How could that be? Who knew he was coming in time to engrave something? He reeled backward. How in the hell...?

Hayley opened the door before he'd even knocked. She was wearing trim designer jeans and a sweater, and she looked like the cat that swallowed the canary. Damn her for the smug smile on her face.

"What the hell is this?" he asked, pointing to the plaque.

"It's your name. It's your office. Do you like it?"

"It looks permanent," he said with a frown.

"Oh, no," she said lightly. "I'll have it sanded off and another name put in. As soon as we get our permanent doctor."

"How did you find the time to have it made? Don't tell me you were so confident you had it engraved before you even left for San Francisco?"

"Let's just say I was hopeful," she said, her eyes sparkling. She'd won and she knew it. "Come in and look around. I made some changes after Grandpa died. He would never let me touch a thing."

"Stubborn old coot," Sam muttered.

"Think what you want, but he was the last of the old-time doctors. Made house calls and never turned anyone away."

"Not even me," Sam said under his breath.

"Hello, Sam," the nurse said. She was sitting behind her desk against the far wall as if she hadn't moved in sixteen years. Maybe she hadn't. Her tone was as frosty as ever, her uniform just as starchy. She'd put on a few pounds, but her expression was the same, stiff and stern and definitely disapproving. He felt as if he was eighteen again, coming in to be patched up for one last time.

"Hello, Ms. Whitlock."

"I never expected to see you here again," Mattie said.

"That makes two of us," he said.

"Think you can take Doc's place, do you?" she asked.

"Now, Mattie," Hayley cautioned. "No one will ever take Grandpa's place. But Sam has very graciously, very generously agreed to fill in for him. For a while."

Gracious…generous? That was typical Hayley. Putting a positive spin on everything. Refusing to recognize reality. Except for one thing. The reality that the town bad boy from the wrong side of the tracks could *not* end up with the town princess and live happily ever after.

"For a short while," he said firmly. "I'll be out of here and out of your hair in six months."

"Humph," Mattie said with a sniff. "What made you come back at all?"

Sam glanced at Hayley, who gave an almost imperceptible shrug. Was it possible that she and her grandfather were the only ones who knew about the scholarship? He hoped so.

"The fresh air. The fishing. The golf. The friendly people," he said.

Mattie raised her eyebrows. "I'm no stranger to sarcasm, young man," she said. "I suppose Hayley told you I'll be your assistant. Where you come from you probably have a group of medical students you can order around. And a team of residents. I've seen how it is on those TV doctor shows. But that's not the way it is here. And don't think I'm always going to be available to help you out. In fact, I only work half days on account of my heart."

"What's wrong with your heart?" he asked.

"Nothing," she snapped. "I just don't want to strain it."

"You work half days, I'll work the other half," Hayley interjected.

Sam turned to look at her, and so did the nurse.

"You?" they chorused.

"Yes, me. Of course I don't have the training or the experience that you do, Mattie, but I might be able to do the billing and...whatever else is needed."

Sam glared at her. No. He didn't want her in the office, distracting him, trying to help out. Reminding him he was there under duress. Of course, he didn't want old stoneface around, either. He just wished it didn't have to be either of them. But he was going to need someone. It was true. He had medical students to do his scut work. Interns who made rounds with him and hung on every word he said. And he hadn't the slightest idea how to run an office.

"Well," Hayley said brightly, "let's take a tour, Sam. I'm afraid the equipment is sadly out-of-date," she said as they went from the waiting room to the office to the examining room. "Just give me a list of what you'll need, and I'll order it."

"I'll manage," he said gruffly. He knew now why he should never have come. Once again he felt like the poor kid from the wrong side of the tracks being patched up by Doc Bancroft. The kid who couldn't pay his bill, couldn't even leave a sack of apples on the porch.

"It's only for six months," he reminded her and himself. He looked out the back window at a young woman pushing a stroller down Elm Street, and he wondered if he would remember how to deliver a baby, if he'd be telephoned in the middle of the night to reassure anxious parents when their kids were spiking fevers of 104 or having an asthmatic attack. "Maybe no one will come. Maybe they'd rather drive to Portland than put themselves in my hands. Did you ever think of that?" he asked Hayley.

"Don't be ridiculous. Everyone I've talked to is delighted you're going to be here. So delighted the local businesses have put together a welcome basket."

"A welcome basket. Just what I wanted. What's in it? A loaf of bread from the Good Times Bakery where I used to snitch doughnuts before school? An ice cream cone from the soda shop where I got thrown out for looking scruffy, annoying the paying customers and reading their magazines but never buying any?"

"Sam, please. No one remembers these things but you. Or if they do, they're willing to forgive and forget."

"Mattie doesn't look as if she's forgotten or forgiven."

"That's Mattie," she said.

"Maybe I don't give a damn about being forgiven, as long as I can be forgotten," he suggested.

Forgotten. As if she'd ever forgotten that last night in this examining room. The blinds were drawn. The blood was running down Sam's face. Mattie was holding the syringe. She thought she was going to faint when her grandfather laid him on the table, picked up a needle and shot him full of anesthetic. Her heart pounded as the memories came rushing back. She glanced over at Sam, wondering if he was thinking of that night, wishing it hadn't ended the way it had. Wishing she could have prevented what happened, but she couldn't.

She tore her gaze away and led the way into the examining room, nervously adjusting the height of the blinds at the windows, not knowing what to say. Afraid to say anything that would set him off. That would make him turn on his heel and leave. Because under that suave exterior, under the pressed, gray flannel slacks and behind the hand-knit Irish fisherman's sweater he wore, she sensed he was the same proud, poor, combative, stubborn teenage boy she once fell in love with when she was eighteen. All along she'd thought of this deal as benefiting the town. Now she wondered if it might do something for Sam if he'd stay. It might help him overcome his bitterness about the past. If he'd let it. But he probably wouldn't.

"Part of the deal is free housing," she said. As if he cared. As if he couldn't afford to pay.

"That's nice," he said. "But I'm not exactly poor, since I had no debts to pay off...." The way he said it was a verbal nudge to remind her that she'd shamed him into coming. That he had a debt to pay off and that was the only reason he was there.

"I'm sorry about that," she said. "I never meant to tell you. I told you Grandpa never would have let you know, but…"

"But you were desperate."

"Yes. Anyway, since you'll only be here six months, I hope you'll be comfortable at the B&B."

"Where is it?"

"At my house."

"Your house? You've turned your family home into a bed and breakfast? So you really did lose your money. How did that happen? Or is that another 'long story'?"

"No, it's a short story. My father made some bad investments. They left and retired to Arizona where it's dry and warm and better for my mother's arthritis. I managed to hang on to the house. But only just barely. Business hasn't been exactly great. But I'm expecting guests tonight, a family. I hope you don't mind having kids around."

"Do you?" he asked.

"I like kids," she said. "That house was made for a big family. I thought…"

"You thought by now you'd have a few of your own," he said.

She turned her head and swallowed over a lump in her throat. How had the conversation taken this dangerous turn? She wished she'd never mentioned kids. She wished she hadn't ever confided in him and that he didn't have such a good memory. Not so long ago she'd wanted a baby desperately. So desperately she'd married the wrong man and then… "I did, but I'm not married," she explained. "I guess I'm an oddity these days. But I believe every kid should have two parents."

The lines in his forehead deepened, and she wished she could have bitten her tongue. Sam had a mother, but what a mother, and he'd barely known his father. How insensitive of her to say what she'd said.

"Anyway," she continued, "I'm expecting this family, and maybe they'll tell their friends what a wonderful town New Hope is and what a great place the Bancroft House is for families and the word will spread and I'll have more and more guests and—"

"What if you do get more guests? How do you think you're going to run a bed and breakfast and work half-time in the office?" he asked.

"Piece of cake," she said lightly. "If I have more business, I'll hire help."

"I hope you don't think having a doctor in town is going to bring in more tourists. Because I've got news for you. It's probably not going to make a damn bit of difference. You know that, don't you?"

"Of course I know that," she said. "But what about the mill worker who gets a finger caught in the saw? Or the kid who breaks his arm on the school playground or the baby who's running a fever of 105? That's where having a doctor will make a huge difference."

"I'm not a pediatrician or an orthopedic surgeon. I hope you know that."

"I know exactly what you are," she said. But she didn't. Not really. Not anymore. But Lord help her, she wanted to know. Was that the real reason she'd wanted him back? To see if there was anything there between them? Anything worth salvaging? Was she just as selfish as ever, despite her years of helping others? She didn't want to even consider the possibility. But Mattie had considered it. Mattie had made no secret of wondering if Hayley had ulterior motives in going after Sam.

He shot her a skeptical look. A look that said nobody knew what he was. Not even him. "I'm going to take inventory,'' he said. "And see what we've got here. You can go now. And take that ogre in the front office with you.''

"You call Mattie an ogre? What about that woman in your front office? I thought she was going to have me for lunch if I tried to invade your inner sanctum.''

"Marion? She's been with me for two years. Supereffificient. Knows what I need before I ask. Wouldn't hurt a flea. You're too sensitive, Hayley. Now go home and do whatever it is you do for your guests.''

She gave a little sigh of relief. He wasn't leaving. At least not yet. "In the afternoon I put out the sherry and cheese and crackers. I give them tips about where to eat and what to do. In the morning it's breakfast. Scones, hot cereal, fresh fruit, muffins. And more tips.''

"I could use some of those tips. And the muffins. I'm impressed. You couldn't boil water when I knew you.''

"I've changed.'' She ran a hand through her blond hair, suddenly exhausted from trying to act cheerful and normal when she felt anything but. Trying to make him glad he'd come, when he was so obviously not. He wasn't the only one worried about how this scheme would turn out. "So have you,'' she murmured under her breath.

She crossed the room quickly, anxious to get out of there, to put some space between them, but before she could leave he grabbed her arm and pulled her roughly toward him until there were only inches between them. His eyes were so dark and so hard they looked like black obsidian. And there was a faint scar at the corner of his eyebrow. A souvenir of that last night in town. Of the stitches Grandpa put there that saved his eye.

Sam smelled like the wind off the ocean and the leather of his expensive car and again she was scared to death. This time she wasn't scared he'd leave, she was scared he'd stay. Because she didn't know how she was going to work and live under the same roof with him without falling in love all over again.

"This isn't going to work, Hayley," he said through clenched teeth. Which echoed her sentiments exactly.

She met his gaze, trying to play dumb, play innocent. "What isn't?"

"Working together, staying at your house. Do you know how many times I pressed my face against that ten-foot-tall wrought-iron front gate of yours? How many times I wanted to be part of your world?"

"You were part of my world," she whispered. "The most important part."

He held her at arm's length and observed her with cold, unforgiving eyes. "No," he said. "Not when it counted."

Her heart thumped, she felt tears collecting and threatening to spill over. Unable to speak, she jerked out of his grasp, skirted around him and walked past Mattie to the front door, her mind spinning, wondering if she'd really done the right thing after all by persuading him to come. Yes, his presence was needed, yes he might even save lives, but what about her? Who was going to save her? Mattie looked up from her ancient Royal typewriter.

"You were right," the nurse hissed. "He has changed."

"See? I told you," Hayley said, forcing a smile.

"He's even more arrogant than ever, if you ask me," she said with a glance over her shoulder.

Hayley bit her lip to keep from saying, I didn't ask you. Instead she closed the door firmly behind her and went home. If Sam stayed, either he and Mattie would kill each other or they'd achieve some kind of working arrangement. She had to hope for the latter, but she couldn't do any more about it today. Her nerves were shot, her heart was pounding and she dreaded the arrival of Sam at her house.

Why had she ever volunteered to put him up? Why hadn't she found him a room somewhere else? She knew the answer to that one. She just didn't want to admit it. She was still in love with him.

Three

There was a sport utility vehicle parked in the circular driveway in front of the Bancroft House, which was unarguably the biggest, the most beautiful and the most prominent house in town. Sitting on a knoll, with a view of the ocean from every window, it was a monument to the past, a tribute to Hayley's ancestors, the early Bancrofts who'd made their fortune in lumber. Way too big for a single person, even way too big for a family with two children and a grandfather who had lived on the third floor. Hayley still loved living there.

But she couldn't afford to live there much longer unless she earned some money. Turning the house into a bed and breakfast seemed like an obvious solution for a woman with no discernible skills except doing community development in Africa and volunteer work in Portland, cooking and running a house. She'd done the latter for her husband

and got no credit for it, why not do it for profit? Only there was no profit. Not yet.

That was the cry all over New Hope. No business. Young people were leaving for Portland and Seattle. Old people were leaving for L.A. and Phoenix. No, a doctor wasn't going to turn New Hope into Newport, that quaint seaport with the new aquarium and the chic shops. That's not why she'd gone after a doctor. It wouldn't solve all their problems. As Sam had suggested, it was probably not going make a damn bit of difference economically. But if he saved one life, eased one person's pain, then it was worth it, she knew.

"Hi, you must be the Kirks. I'm Hayley Bancroft," she told the woman who was standing in front of the house with a baby nestled against her in a front carrier and the *Guidebook to Oregon Bed and Breakfasts* in her hand. Hayley told herself not to act too eager. Not to act as if they were the first guests she'd seen in two weeks. Maybe they weren't the Kirks after all. Maybe they were lost tourists.

"Is this the Bancroft House?" the woman said.

"Yes, it is," Hayley said with a smile. "And I'm the owner."

"Thank heavens. We've been driving for seven hours. You did say you take kids, didn't you?"

"Of course we do. A baby is no problem. I have a crib and a high chair."

"And baby-sitting is available?"

Hayley hesitated only a moment. "Definitely." She hadn't planned on it, but she'd do it herself. She had nothing else to do.

The woman heaved a sigh of relief and beckoned to her husband, who was still behind the wheel. He got out, slid the door to the back seat open, and two small children jumped out.

Hayley's eyes widened. When she'd said she would baby-sit, she was thinking baby. One baby. "Oh," she said. "Two more. You'll want the two rooms, I think."

"Kids can sleep on the floor," the man said.

"I see," Hayley said, glad she'd replaced the pristine white carpet that used to be on the floor of the master bedroom, where her parents once slept in the four-poster on satin sheets. Where she and her sister were not allowed to enter in case they'd get footprints on the rug or drool on the sheets or put their little fingerprints on the woodwork. Where the walk-in closets held a huge selection of garments for every occasion—boating, golf, deep-sea fishing, parties, bridge. But all that had changed. She'd replaced the white carpet with neutral beige. And the adjoining master bath was now outfitted with a spa. It was her most luxurious accommodation, but one that wasn't forbidden to kids. She would add a crib and give the room to the parents, but she'd put the boys in her sister's old room for no extra charge.

"Come with me," she said, leading the way up the front steps. "I think you'll be very comfortable here."

Sam left the office without saying goodbye to Nurse Whitlock. He had nothing to say to her and he knew the feeling was mutual. She'd made her feelings about his return to town abundantly clear. Not that he cared. He didn't need her approval or anyone else's. She had her back to him when he passed through the waiting room. He stood in front of the office looking up and down the street. He wasn't ready to go to the Bancroft House yet. He might never be ready. He wasn't ready to go back to his old house, either, and he *knew* he would never be ready to do that.

It should have given him satisfaction to think of walking through the iron gate of Hayley's house as a guest, but it didn't. He wanted to forget the past, and he couldn't do that while he was in New Hope. It was all around him, the places and the people he'd pushed to the back of his mind. But how could he leave the painful memories in the past while he worked in Doc Bancroft's office or slept under the same roof as his granddaughter? Six months stretched ahead of him like the long road from here to the California border. He would take it the way he'd taken all the long roads in his life, one step at a time. But it wasn't going to be easy.

He walked up the street toward the diner and went in to have a cup of coffee. Several heads swiveled in his direction as he took a seat at the counter. But nobody said a word except the waitress, a gum-chewing middle-aged woman who called him "hon." Then she did a double take.

"I don't believe it. Didn't think you'd have the nerve to show your face in this town again. You don't remember me, do you, Sam?" she asked as she plunked his coffee in front of him. "Wilma Henwood. Those were my flower beds you ran over with your motorcycle."

He racked his brain but couldn't remember any flower beds. But it wasn't hard to imagine he'd done it. That and much worse. "I'm sorry about that. I'd be happy to replace them for you."

"It's a little late. Twenty years to be exact."

"I guess it is. I'd still like to do it."

"What do you think of New Hope these days?"

"It's changed," he said.

"So've you," she said, tilting her head to one side to

observe him. "Hear you're a doctor now. Taking Doc Bancroft's place."

"Only temporarily."

"Can't blame you. Those are pretty big shoes to fill."

Sam pressed his lips together to keep from saying that wasn't why he was only temporary.

"Where you staying?" she asked.

He was surprised she didn't know. The way gossip spread in this town. "At the Bancroft House."

"She's got it fixed up real nice. I went through it last Christmas on the house tour to make money for the library. Not that there was anything wrong with it to begin with. Still, her folks had different ideas about style than Hayley does. She's more the unpretentious type, don't you think? What do you think of her?" she asked, while she refilled a salt shaker.

"She's changed."

"Pretty as ever, though," she said.

"Very pretty," he agreed.

"Too bad about her divorce."

"Yeah, too bad." He didn't want to hear about her marriage or her divorce.

"The creep walked out on her," Wilma said. "Just because—"

"How's the pie?" he asked, attempting to change the subject.

"No complaints so far," Wilma said. "Get you a piece?"

He nodded. When he and Hayley had shared confidences so long ago, he'd talked about getting out of New Hope and bragged about making a ton of money and thumbing his nose at the world. But Hayley had always talked about a future right there in town with a husband and kids. As if it was a given. Why not? She'd always gotten everything else she'd wanted. He wondered what had gone wrong. Who had she married? Was it anyone he'd known? Whoever it was, it must have been some time ago. She didn't appear to be suffering now. And if she was, she wouldn't share it with him.

"It's her parents I feel sorry for," Wilma said, jerking him out of his reverie.

"How's that?" Sam couldn't imagine wasting an iota of sympathy on Georgia and Franklin Bancroft. They were rich and snobbish, and they'd forbidden Hayley to see him. Of course, he was hardly the type of boy they wanted their daughter going out with. Face it, who would want their daughter going out with him? *He* wouldn't want his daughter going out with someone like him. Someone with an attitude like his. With parents like his. With a sketchy past and a bleak future.

"Lost their money. Bad investments."

"Oh, that." He took a bite of pie.

"Still got that motorcycle?" she asked.

"No," he said. He neglected to inform her that instead of the old, beat-up Yamaha he'd picked up at the wrecking yard outside town, he now had a new Honda CB1000 that would do 160 on the open road. If he ever got out to the open road. So far he hadn't had time to ride it. Just knowing he could afford it, knowing it was there in case he had time was enough. It was now parked in the garage at his apartment building, awaiting his return, which couldn't come a moment too soon to suit him.

"You married?" she asked, wiping the counter clean.

"No." Why had he ever come in here today? He wasn't ready to be grilled by the biggest gossip in town. He would never be ready for that.

"Neither is Hayley," she said pointedly.

"So you said."

"Never cared much for her parents, did you?"

"Never knew them very well," he said. Actually he knew them as well as he wanted to. His first encounter with Mrs. Bancroft came at about age ten when he'd been passing by their house dragging a stick along their fence...ka-ching, ka-chin, ka-ching, wondering what it would be like to be rich enough to live in a house like that. Vowing that someday he'd have enough money to have such a showplace. That someday he'd be as respectable as they were. As he daydreamed, idly banging his stick, the Bancroft poodle started barking, and Hayley's mother got up off her lawn chair.

"Stop that," she screamed. He wasn't sure if she was yelling at him or the dog. In any case, he continued walking around the perimeter of their property, whistling and banging his stick while the dog continued frantically barking at him from the other side of the fence and Mrs. Bancroft became apopleptic. That was indicative of the way things went between him and the Bancrofts from then on.

Sam laid a bill on the counter and stood up. "Nice to see you, Mrs. Henwood. I haven't forgotten about your flowers."

"Guess we'll be seeing more of you around here," she said. "Hayley doesn't do dinners, only breakfasts."

He nodded. Every night at the diner with meat loaf, mashed potatoes or chicken-fried steak? Every night more interrogation? More gossip? For six months?

When he finally did pass through the gate and walk up to the wraparound front porch of the dove-gray Victorian mansion, he steeled himself for a rush of unwanted memories, but he didn't feel anything. Not even satisfaction or revenge, nothing. He was numb. Until Hayley met him at the door with a baby in her arms. Then the shock waves rolled through him. His pulse rate rose. He took a step backward and stared at her as if he'd never seen her before. He hadn't. Not like that.

Four

It wasn't Hayley's baby. It couldn't be. She wasn't married. She believed in the traditional family. Mother, father and kids. And yet, the way she was standing there in her doorway, holding it as if it were hers, as if she was Mrs. America waiting for her husband to come home from work... Then it hit him like a Douglas fir four-by-twelve. Though he'd never had any family life to speak of, he suddenly knew this was what it was like. To come home from work and find your wife waiting for you with your baby in her arms. It wasn't something he'd ever wanted.

Growing up in an unhappy home, deserted by the parents who should have cared for him, he was far from a traditionalist and had no illusions about marriage. All he knew was that it wasn't for him and he wanted no part of it. As much as he'd envied the Bancrofts their house and their money, he knew marriage and family were out of the picture. As it happened, his demanding career gave him the perfect excuse for not even contemplating such a scenario.

But for one moment he was seized by an irrational feeling of longing so strong and so painful he could only stand there and gape. He felt a sharp sense of regret for what might have been if Hayley wasn't who she was and he wasn't who he was. He was having a hard enough time getting used to the idea of Hayley as a grown woman, let alone as a wife or a mother. He didn't know what to say.

"Where…how…who?" he asked.

"They're here," she said. "The family I told you about." She stepped back and shifted the baby higher on her shoulder, blithely unaware of the impression she'd created. "I forgot that I'd advertised baby-sitting services. The parents checked in, drank a glass of sherry then took off."

"And left you with their baby?"

"That's not all," she said glancing over her shoulder at two small boys dressed like Power Rangers, sitting on the floor watching TV. "I can't complain. I asked for it. I wanted guests. I offered baby-sitting. I just didn't expect them to be so…so noisy and have so much energy. I thought I'd tuck them in bed and read them a story, but they don't want to go to bed. They don't want to hear any 'baby stories,' either."

"Look out, it's Godzilla," one shrieked, catching a glimpse of Sam out of the corner of his eye.

His brother jumped up and placed a rocket in a miniature launcher which he aimed straight at Sam. Sam ducked and the rocket hit the bay window with a loud bang. The window cracked but didn't break. Hayley gasped and there was a moment of shocked silence.

The boys then dropped their power launcher and ran out of the room, screaming excitedly at the top of their lungs.

The baby burst into tears. Hayley patted her back. She cried louder.

"Oh, Lord, what have I done?" Hayley asked, looking at the window with dismay. "I should never have offered to take care of those monsters. I don't know anything about babies. I don't know anything about kids. And I can't afford to replace that window."

"It was my fault. They took me by surprise. Never thought I looked like Godzilla. But it's the kind of thing I used to do, firing rockets at the enemy. Catch them off guard. I should have taken the hit instead of the window. I shouldn't have ducked," Sam said, examining the crack in the glass.

"You have good reflexes," she said. "But you're not required to take the hit. You're not the secret service," she said morosely.

"I owe it to you. I cracked a window in this house one time."

"I don't remember that," she lied, nuzzling the baby with her cheek. But she remembered only too well. The sharp crack as a stone hit her bedroom window in the middle of the night. The shock as a rush of cold air hit her when she opened the window in her nightgown. The sight of Sam in his black leather jacket looking up at her. Her whole body shook with fright. She'd been scared her parents would hear. Scared he wouldn't leave. Scared he would.

"In this case I'd say the parents are responsible for replacing it," Sam said.

"Then they'll never come back here, and they won't recommend it to their friends. No, I can't even tell them. Where do you think they went?"

"The parents?" he asked.

"No, the little devils."

"I'll go look," he said, crossing the room. "I understand how their minds work. I'll find them."

"And when you do—"

"I'll bury them alive in your mother's rose garden. No one will think of looking there."

Despite the broken window, the screams and the cries, she smiled. Glad to see he hadn't lost his roguish sense of humor. "Actually the garden isn't a bad idea, if you could get them out there. There's still a tire hanging from the oak tree. But you shouldn't have to," she said feeling a pang of guilt for using him this way, on his first day in town. "You're a guest, after all."

"No problem," he said. "Playhouse still there?" he asked casually.

Hayley jerked her head up from the baby's cheek. "Yes," she said. "Although it was renovated, turned into a pool house some time after...after I left home, but basically...I mean it's still there."

"Yeah, uh-huh," he said blandly, and left the living room.

Could he have forgotten? How could he not remember the most important, the most incredible event of her life that had taken place in that garden, in that playhouse? Because to him it didn't mean that much. That's how. The baby's cries subsided to mere snuffles. Hayley looked into its little scrunched-up red face. "Don't cry," she murmured. "Never cry over men. It's not worth it. How about some milk?" she asked. Without waiting for an answer, Hayley headed for the remodeled kitchen and warmed the bottle the parents had left behind.

Then she sat in the garage-sale rocking chair she'd refinished and fed the baby. From where she sat she could see Sam and the two boys running around the yard playing some kind of game involving a ball. He ducked, he darted, he kicked and he ran. What a shame he hadn't played sports in high school. But he'd said they were for kids, and in some ways Sam had never been a kid. Not until now, she thought, watching him gently tackle one of the boys.

So that's what it would be like to have a family of her own, she thought as she rocked slowly back and forth, lulling herself into a dream world. Instead of guests, that would be the kids and the dad in the yard. The mom and the baby in the kitchen. A fire in the wood stove radiating heat. A lamb ragout simmering on the back burner of the restaurant-size stove. A loaf of bread in the oven. Only the last parts were true. She'd started the bread and thrown the stew together this afternoon, just in case, hoping Sam would stay for dinner, knowing she shouldn't count on him… but hoping…wanting to make him feel at home, though he wasn't looking for a home, not with her, anyway.

She suspected this was as close as she'd get to a real family life. The baby in her arms was not hers, the kids in the yard were not hers, the man out there was not hers, either. A family was not in the cards for her. She'd tried and it didn't work. She would probably never know the satisfaction of feeding her own baby or of rocking it in this chair. But she had so much else—friends, the house— that she couldn't complain.

The baby fell asleep in her arms and she walked upstairs and put her in the crib she'd set up in the master bedroom suite, pressing her lips against its soft baby cheek for just a moment before laying it into the crib. Then she went back to the kitchen and stirred the stew. Dusk was falling on the old house, a fine mist was blowing off the bay. She looked out the window and saw Sam standing in the yard looking at her. It was too dark to see his face, but she could feel the heat from his gaze all the way in here. Just like that night so long ago.

She stood for a moment looking out at him, wishing, wondering... Transported back in time. To that night when she'd stood in the window shivering, her heart hammering under her thin nightgown that billowed around her body. He'd threatened to climb the drain pipe and come up. She contemplated sliding down the drainpipe. Just to keep him from coming up.

Her memories faded as they burst into the kitchen, the wild children and the high-priced doctor who'd spent the last half hour playing with them.

"We're hungry," the small boy with the freckles announced.

"How about some lamb stew?" she asked brightly.

"Yuck," the boys chorused.

"Have you got any peanut butter?" Sam asked.

"For you?"

"No, for them. I'll have a glass of your sherry. They're all yours." He left the kitchen and headed for the living room and the imported sherry while Hayley spread peanut butter on bread, poured two glasses of milk and seated the boys at the breakfast table.

When they finished, she set them up in the den with a video their parents had thoughtfully provided and which Hayley hoped didn't contain any violence that would incite them to do further damage to her house. Then she went back to the living room to find Sam.

He was sitting on the couch in semidarkness with a tumbler of amber liquid in his hand staring out at the lights on the bay. Before she could speak he set his glass down and rubbed his hands together.

"I didn't mean for you to play baby-sitter," she said.

He shrugged. "I'm out of shape. Haven't played touch

football in years. Not since college. Of course it wasn't really fair, two against one,'' he said, smiling.

''How's your hand?'' she asked, sitting on the far end of the couch. Far enough away to remove any temptation. On her part, not his. He wasn't even looking at her, instead his gaze was fastened somewhere on the horizon.

''It's all right. Why? Oh, you heard about my run-in with the door.'' He clenched and unclenched his fist, testing it. ''That was nothing.''

''That's good. I imagine most things you do require two good hands.''

''Not everything,'' he said. ''I can think of a few things that don't. A few things I could do with one.'' His voice was low and rough and loaded with meaning. He turned to look at her then, a long, slow, intimate look that made her pulse quicken, and she wished she hadn't started this conversation.

Sounds of the video came from the study, mingled with muted shouts and laughter. She hoped it was too dark for him to see her face flame, she hoped he couldn't hear her heart pound as she contemplated the things that could be done with one hand. With his hand. A surgeon's hand. Touching, exploring, exciting...which was probably just what he wanted her to contemplate. He was no longer a hormone-driven, sexy, dangerous bad boy. No, he was a hormone-driven, sexy, dangerous man.

No, she was not going to fall for Sam again. She was too smart, and she'd been through too much. But she couldn't tear her gaze away. Not when he looked at her like that. Like he knew what she was thinking, what effect he had on her. She continued to stare at him, trying to see beyond the face and the attitude. Trying to see what kind of man Sam Prentice had become.

One thing hadn't changed. They were from two different

worlds. Only now his was the world of high-powered, high-priced medicine. Her world was back in the small town she called home, where she was struggling to make a living.

"What about eating?" she asked lightly, finally breaking the spell. "You can do that with one hand. I can offer you lamb stew or the house special, peanut butter sandwiches."

"I'll take whatever smells so good."

She got up off the couch, comfortable in her role as hostess, and led the way into the brightly lit kitchen.

"I thought you didn't do dinners," he said as she set a large bowl of savory ragout in front of him.

"Where did you hear that?"

"I stopped in at the diner."

"Don't tell me. You saw Wilma. What else did she tell you about me?" she asked with a frown. She knew it would happen sooner or later. The gossip, the stories.

"Nothing. Sit down. I hate to eat alone."

She poured herself a bowl of stew and sat down. "Who do you usually eat with?" she asked, picturing him with beautiful women at expensive restaurants.

"Peter Jennings or Tom Brokaw. What about you?"

"I prefer Dan Rather," she said.

"To me?" he asked with a glint in his eye. He thought he knew the answer to that one. He thought she would choose him. He was as cocky as ever. She had to keep up her guard so he wouldn't know that his effect on her was as devastating as ever. His ego didn't need any more inflating.

She paused with a forkful of lamb in midair. "I'm not sure. I don't know you, Sam. You've changed and I have, too. I don't know what to think. I'm having trouble adjusting to the new you."

"How do you think I feel?" he asked. "I hadn't thought about you for years. You drop in on my life and suddenly I'm back in New Hope. I'm in your house, eating dinner with you. It blows my mind."

She nodded understandingly. But the idea he hadn't thought about her for years hurt. Especially since she'd never been able to totally forget about him. There was a long silence. She sliced some bread. He took a piece.

"How did you learn to cook like this?" he asked. "Or is that one of the things you can't talk about?"

"I took some classes," she said, ignoring his last question.

"I didn't think you learned at home," he said.

"Oh, no. Mother didn't want my sister and me in the kitchen ever. She was sure when we grew up we'd have someone else cook our food just as she did. To her it was like learning to type. If you did, you'd be consigned to being a secretary. If you learned to cook, you'd end up in the kitchen. She couldn't have foreseen the demise of the Bancroft fortune. Now I imagine even she has to cook occasionally, unless they go out to dinner every night." She took a sip of water. "I assume that's your life, too, restaurants or dinner parties. A successful surgeon, a bachelor, you must be in some demand on the social scene." She kept her tone light. She didn't want him to think she was prying. He'd always hated answering questions about his home life. Because he didn't have one. And she didn't want him to think she cared if he was on the town every night with some beautiful woman, because she didn't.

"I was when I first hit town," he said. "So I made the rounds, maybe just to prove I could. That I was good enough. A dirty, scrappy kid from the wrong side of town. But I don't play that game anymore. And most women don't want to deal with my surgery schedule. So I usually end up having dinner with Tom Brokaw, if I have dinner at all. In case you're interested, I prefer you to him.''

She set her fork down. The look in his eyes sent chills up and down her spine, while her face was burning. How could he do that to her after all these years? One back-handed compliment and she was eighteen again, crazy in love again, her hormones raging.

She reminded herself that she'd dated, she'd been married, and yet there was no other man who had ever made her feel that way. With just a few words and a look. Making her feel like the most desirable woman in the world. As if he'd pursue her to the ends of the earth. Which he hadn't…wouldn't. He hadn't ever been back to ask about her. Hadn't even thought about her in all these years.

''I'd better go see how those boys are doing,'' she said briskly, getting to her feet. ''Maybe I can get them to bed.''

''Want some help?''

''No. You stay where you are. You're a guest and you've already done your time.''

Sam ate slowly, enjoying the savory stew, looking around the kitchen at the maple countertops, the copper pots hanging from a rack over the sink, the delft-blue tea-pot and a bunch of garden flowers stuck into a vintage milk bottle. He wondered how much she'd done to the room and how much was a remainder of the glory days of the Bancrofts. He recalled what Wilma had said. ''She's got it fixed up real nice.… Her folks let it go downhill.'' Yes, she did have it fixed up real nice. It had a certain charm to it. A warmth, a welcoming spirit. Like Hayley herself.

The house was quiet now. Only the chiming of the grandfather clock in the front hall on the quarter hour broke the stillness. What had she done with the kids? The only way those kids would be quiet was if they were asleep or unconscious. He knew, because he was once that kind of kid.

He walked up the wide staircase with the polished oak railing that, if he were eight years old, he wouldn't have been able to resist sliding down. But he was thirty-four, a mature adult. At the top of the stairs he hesitated. So many rooms. When he heard giggling and smothered whispers, he followed the sound down the hall, opened a door to see two sleeping bags on the floor with tousled heads poking out of them.

Like mummies coming to life the boys raised their heads and looked at him. "Hey, Godzilla," one said. "You got something wrong with your hand?"

He looked down at his knuckles, still sore and bruised. He didn't think anyone would notice, hadn't realized he was favoring it, but the kids were more observant than he'd thought. "It was bitten off by an alligator so I had it replaced with a bionic hand."

"No kidding?" the youngest asked. "Did it hurt?"

Sam held up his hand and flexed his fingers. Yeah, it hurt. "Nah. This one's made of titanium and kryptonite."

"Can we touch it?"

"Nope. You might get contaminated. Then you couldn't live on earth. I'd have to take you to Krypton with me."

"Cool."

"Go to sleep," Sam said, and closed the door behind him.

Now where was Hayley?

He walked quietly down the hall, sinking into deep, plush carpet, opening bedroom doors as he went. Guest rooms, he assumed, wondering which was his—the one with the dark hardwood furniture or the one with the sea-scapes on the wall or the one with twin beds and bookcases lining the wall. It couldn't be the one with the handmade quilt and the pale curtains with the hint of wild rose perfume in the air. That had to be Hayley's. He stood in the doorway feeling guilty for spying, feeling drawn to her, to her room, to her house, to everything about her.

He should never have come here. She only wanted him for one thing—for his medical degree. To fill in for her grandfather. To do a few procedures, set a few broken bones, deliver a baby or two. Until she found someone who'd stick around. He was as wrong now for this town and for her as he'd ever been. But tonight, when he was sitting across the table from her at dinner, he had trouble remembering this. He wondered, not for the first time, how he was going to get through the next six months.

The last door on the right turned out to be the master bedroom suite. There were huge gabled windows, a padded window seat, a chaise lounge, a massive, king-size bed covered with an elegant embroidered comforter. At the foot of the bed stood an old-fashioned wicker crib.

Hayley stood at the side of the crib looking down at the sleeping baby with a wistful expression on her face. He frowned, wondering why she wasn't still married and why she hadn't had kids. He had some other questions for her, too, but they'd have to wait. After all, he had six months.

Hayley glanced up when she heard his footsteps and put her index finger against her lips. He crossed the room and stood next to her, watching the pink-cheeked baby sleep, its tiny fingers clenched into fists. She gripped the edge of the crib so tightly her knuckles turned white. Standing there he sensed her longing, her deep-felt desire to have a baby of her own. He could be all wrong. How did he know that was what she wanted? He didn't know her anymore. Maybe that wasn't it at all.

After all, he had no desire to be a father. How could he

be? He'd never had a father to speak of. Had no idea what they were supposed to do. He knew what they *weren't* supposed to do. Use physical punishment. Or verbal abuse. Withhold financial support. Drink and gamble away earnings. Walk out on your family. And those were just for starters.

"Okay," she said softly, turning away reluctantly. "We can go now. I just wanted to see if she was asleep."

"You wouldn't want one of those, would you?" he asked when they'd reached the bottom of the stairs.

"A baby? Of course not. I haven't got time for a baby. Babies are a lot of work."

"A lot of trouble," he agreed.

"They cry," she said, pouring herself a glass of sherry from the decanter in the living room. "They throw up and they have diarrhea."

"And colic," he added.

"I've heard," she said. "What about you? Don't you want to have kids?"

"No way. I wouldn't know what to do with kids."

"You knew what to do with these tonight."

"For one night. My dad was good for one night, too. One night about twenty-five years ago. Which was more than enough. That was it. Then he took off. I never saw him again. Thank God."

Hayley gave him a swift glance, then looked away, but not before he saw the sympathy welling up in her eyes, the pity that he hated, no matter who it came from. The kind that made him want to reach out and punch someone. Or kiss them. He studied her mouth, her full lower lip, and it took all his willpower to keep from grabbing her by the shoulders and pressing his mouth against hers until the pity was replaced by passion. White-hot passion. Until she opened up to him, responding the way she'd once done, with all the eagerness and excitement of the girl she once was and the woman she'd become; until she put her arms around him and he felt her body merge with his, her soft curves pressed against him. He wanted, *needed,* to erase the sympathy from her eyes. To replace it with lust and longing. To show her there was unfinished business between them. As if she didn't know.

Hayley turned her head away and set her glass on the mantel firmly, deliberately, scrupulously avoiding his gaze as if she knew what he was thinking. "I'd better show you your room," she said.

He got his suitcase from his car, and they went back upstairs. This time she took him down the hall to a large room next to hers with a window facing the water. The pictures on the wall were black-and-white photographs of Africa. There was a mosquito netting draped over the four-poster bed and a thick sheepskin rug on the hardwood floor. He set his suitcase next to the door and crossed the room to examine a shelf full of carved wooden animals. He ran his hand over a dark, polished wooden elephant, so solid, so smooth to the touch.

"My souvenirs," she explained.

"Ever see any of these in real life?" he asked.

She shook her head. "No, I guess that's why I bought the carvings. I always wanted to go on safari, but that's not what I was there for. They gave us a living allowance, but not enough for anything extra."

"I had a patient from Africa once. Congenital heart defect. I patched him up and sent him home. He was so grateful he invited me to visit him and go to the game reserve."

"Did you go?" she asked eagerly.

"No. I couldn't take the time. I haven't taken a vacation

for years. Maybe never. If I'd gone I might have seen you," he said, with a hint of a smile.

"Probably not. It's awfully big, Africa."

"So I hear." He set the elephant down. "Ah, well…" He looked out the window, his expression bland, but his eyes dark and sad. For one brief moment Hayley thought he might have regrets about not seeing her in all these years. But she knew better. If he had regrets at all they would be about his single-minded pursuit of a career. And if he did, she'd probably never hear them. His regrets at present probably centered on coming back to New Hope.

"I suppose you're wondering what you're going to do for the next six months when you're not working eighty-hour weeks," she said, hoping to change the subject.

"Aside from golf and digging for clams? No, I haven't thought that far ahead. If I did I might take a running leap off the far end of the dock. Right now I'm concerned with what I'm going to do for the next few hours."

The harsh tone of his voice hit her like a splash of cold water off that same dock. "Look, Sam, maybe this was a big mistake," she blurted. "I…I didn't think it through enough. If you really hate it here so much and you want to go, I can't keep you here."

"Unfortunately I have no place *to* go," he said. "I'm just beginning to realize how focused my life has been on medicine. To the exclusion of everything else."

"But isn't that the way it is? The trade-off is you're a wonderful surgeon. You save lives. My God, I think anyone would want what you have."

"Would you?" he asked.

"I…I don't know."

"I didn't think so," he said.

She couldn't protest. As much as she'd like to be in a position to heal the sick, make people well, she wouldn't give up her own life, her own experiences, even the painful ones. After an awkward silence she got back to the subject of Sam's lack of things to do, places to go.

"Unfortunately there isn't much to do in town on a weeknight," she said apologetically. As if he didn't know.

"And on the weekends?" he asked.

"Well...not really. No, I take that back. There are some festivals coming up this summer. The kite-flying contest for one. On the bluffs."

"I'll look forward to that," he said.

She sent him a sharp glance. "As Mattie would say, I'm no stranger to sarcasm," she said.

He looked at his watch. "I'll go out and drive around for a while."

After a seventeen-hour drive up the coast, he must be really desperate to want to go out and drive some more. She wished she could think of something to suggest, aside from the Red Barn, a seedy bar outside of town, or a game of Scrabble with her by the fire. Either was apt to earn her another sarcastic remark. Which she didn't need.

Hayley walked down the stairs with him without speaking and watched him thrust his arms into the sleeves of his leather jacket.

"See you later," she said as he walked out to his car. He didn't turn around. Not a word, not even a wave of his hand. She wouldn't see him later, of course, if he didn't come back, which was quite possible. Although he'd left his suitcase in the room. Which didn't necessarily mean anything. She'd been left before. Walked out on. Deserted. She knew the signs. She knew the feeling. Though by the time her husband left, she didn't feel anything. She still didn't want to go through it again. Ever.

She walked through the house, dimming the lights, feeling more alone than she had since she'd returned to New

Hope three years ago and moved into the house. Just because she'd shared a few hours with a man she barely knew anymore. It was ridiculous. She wasn't alone. She was with three children, and their parents were due back any time. This was what she wanted. To have the house full of guests. Now she suddenly didn't want that anymore. She wanted a house full of a husband and children.

Dream on, she told herself. She'd tried it and it didn't work. There was no husband material in New Hope, and she wasn't going to leave her town. She had to forget her impossible dreams and get real. And be happy with what she had. If Sam hadn't come, she'd never even have thought about what she didn't have. It was his fault for making her want more.

She loaded the dishwasher, then filled the sink with warm, soapy water and scrubbed the pots so vigorously she almost rubbed the copper off the bottoms. The parents came home. She assured them their children were angels. She offered them coffee and liqueurs but they declined. They'd gone to Newport to eat at a well-known seafood restaurant. She wanted to ask if they'd seen a doctor in a Porsche wearing a cable-knit sweater with a bruised hand and an attitude. But she didn't. They went to bed and Hayley sat by the fireplace watching the embers burn down to ash. She wasn't waiting for Sam. Oh, no. That would be stupid. Pointless.

She told herself he would come back. He was no longer an impulsive teenager. He was a responsible adult. If he was going to leave he'd tell her first. But she couldn't help pacing back and forth in front of the window, watching, waiting and wondering.

It started to rain, and she forced herself to go upstairs to bed. She lay in her bed, sitting up every time she heard a car on the wet street. She watched the minutes tick by.

She was exhausted, but still she couldn't sleep. As soon as she did, she woke suddenly to the sound of something clinking against her window. She jumped out of bed and drew back the curtains. And there he was, standing in the front yard just as he had that night so long ago, throwing stones at her window. Only this time it was pouring. He must be soaked through. She shivered as the wind whipped her hair across her cheek and blew her nightgown against her body.

Five

"**H**ey," he shouted. "The door's locked. I don't have a key."

She pressed her hand against her mouth. How could she have forgotten to give him a key? What kind of hostess makes her guest stay out in the rain? Without stopping to put a robe on, she ran down the hall, took the stairs two at a time and skidded in her bare feet to the front door.

Breathless, she flung it open, and he stood there on the porch in the dark looking at her for a long moment, his wet hair hanging over his forehead.

"I'm sorry. I meant to give you a key. Have you been out here long?" she asked.

"Long enough," he said shaking the water off his head. "You must be a sound sleeper. The last time it took you only a few seconds."

The last time. So long ago. And yet the memory was sharp and clear in her mind. "You're soaked," she said.

He took off his wet jacket and hung it on the coatrack. "Have you got any of that sherry left?"

"Of course. Or would you rather have a hot toddy?"

"If you'll have one with me," he said, his gaze traveling slowly over her body.

"I'll just get my robe," she said, suddenly aware she was only wearing a cotton batiste nightgown with nothing underneath it.

"Wait." His voice dropped an octave. He didn't touch her, didn't grab her arm or even put his hand on her shoulder, but she couldn't move. They stood in the hallway under the Tiffany lamp staring at each other. His face was half in shadow and he looked dark and dangerous. He *was* dangerous. Dangerous to her mental health, dangerous to her well-being. Hayley couldn't breathe. The air had been sucked out of her lungs.

She knew he was going to kiss her. It was the look in his eyes. The set of his jaw. The tension in the atmosphere. So thick she could cut it with her mother's silver cake knife. She wanted him to kiss her. She wanted to fling her arms around his neck and pull him so close she could feel his heartbeat. To feel the solid muscles in his chest. And let her fingers sift through his thick, dark hair. She wanted to feel the rainwater from his jacket soak through her nightgown.

But he didn't. Instead he reached behind him and banged the door shut so loudly it sounded like an explosion. Her heart banged against her ribs. She turned and ran up the stairs like a frightened rabbit to get her robe. But who was she frightened of? Not Sam. She was frightened of her own runaway imagination. She'd imagined that Sam wanted to kiss her.

She didn't have to worry about Sam. He'd had a couple of opportunities to come on to her. But he hadn't. Obviously he didn't want to. Because he really wasn't interested. It was a hard pill to swallow, but Sam was used to dispensing pills, and she'd better get used to swallowing them. He was full of himself, aware of his charm and a flirt to boot. That was all. That was enough. He'd always known how to push her buttons. He still did.

He was sitting on a stool at the breakfast bar when she came down, plaid flannel robe firmly belted around her waist. He looked up from the tourist booklet on the Oregon coast he was leafing through. And undressed her with a sexy, mesmerizing gaze that made her knees weak. She might as well have worn nothing at all, for the protection her robe gave her. Because he seemed to see right through it. What was he trying to do? Provoke her? Drive her crazy? She knew he felt nothing for her. She told herself to get over it. Or she'd get her heart broken all over again.

"Plaid flannel. You didn't have to do that for me," he said, studying the lapels that formed a vee between her breasts.

"I didn't," she said primly. "I run a bed and breakfast. I can't run around in a negligee."

"Too bad. Sorry about waking you up," he said, but he didn't look sorry.

"Sorry about locking you out," she said. She reached for a bottle of rum and poured some into a pot and added some spices, grateful to have something to do besides analyze Sam. "Did you find someplace to go?" she asked. She didn't want him to think she was prying, but she had to fill the silence somehow. She was afraid of silence between them. Afraid of her thoughts, her runaway emotions. Of what she might say or what she might do. Something she'd regret later.

"Yeah," he said.

There it was. Silence. She racked her brain but couldn't think of another thing to say.

"I drove out to the Red Barn," he said.

"For a drink?" she asked. Of course he went for a drink. You didn't go to the Red Barn for a hot chocolate or any other reason. Not at this hour. There was no pool table. Nothing but a big, empty barn with sawdust and cigarette butts on the floor and a sour smell in the air.

"No. For old times' sake. My old man hung out there. I hated that place with a vengeance. I went back to see if I could stand to go in."

"Could you?"

Sam shook his head. He'd stood out in front of the bar, the fluorescent outline of a beer bottle in the window, the distorted sound of an ancient jukebox filling the night air. The rain ran down his face and soaked his jacket. But he couldn't bring himself to open the door.

"I was afraid," he said. "Can you believe that? I'm thirty-four years old, for God's sake. My father's got to be dead by now. And I'm afraid to walk into a bar. Afraid I'll see him in there, roaring drunk and shouting obscenities like the night my mother sent me to get him. I'm afraid of a dead man."

He reached for the cup Hayley held out, without looking at her. He didn't want to see the expression on her face. He hadn't meant to tell her what had happened tonight. But somehow it had come out anyway. If she despised him for his cowardice so be it. If she pitied him, let her.

He couldn't keep his feelings bottled up any longer. There was no one else he could talk to. No one else he wanted to talk to. No one knew him as she did. She'd once said she loved him anyway. Which she must have regretted as soon as she'd said it. Or at least regretted it when he ran away. At eighteen, who knows what love is? He cer-

tainly didn't. Growing up without love, he could only
imagine it. He took a drink of the hot beverage and felt it
sting his throat as the warmth traveled through his body.

"Thanks," he said, setting his glass down. "I didn't
mean to blather on like that. To put a burden on you.
Forget I said anything. It must have been…oh, hell, I don't
know why I did it, I don't know what's wrong with me."

She put her hands on his shoulders. He didn't move.
She pulled him so close he buried his face between her
breasts. She was warm, she was soft and he'd missed her
all these years with a fierce longing, and he hadn't even
known what he was missing. His heart thudded. He stifled
a moan. He reached for the belt of her robe and untied it
with sure, steady fingers. Underneath was a nightgown of
the sheerest, softest cotton. Underneath that, the softest,
smoothest skin he'd ever touched. And the memories came
flooding back. A rainy day a long time ago. A dash
through the rain to the back gate of the Bancroft House
where they found shelter in the playhouse. Where their
pent-up teenage passion exploded.

But that was then. This was now. They were grown-ups
now. With experience and judgment. And self-control.
And needs that only seemed to have intensified with the
years. He lifted her nightgown, and splayed his hands
across her back, inhaled her scent, the smell that clung to
her skin. And gave in to the frustration of seeing but not
touching her for the past eight hours, for the past seventeen
years, by running his hands across her hips and over the
curve of her sweet little butt. He'd thought he could last
longer than one day. He'd thought he could make it
through the six months without giving in to temptation.
But he couldn't. Not when she was so warm, so sweet, so
giving. He stood and shoved her robe to the floor, and
lifted her nightgown over her head.

She stood in the middle of the kitchen, completely naked and so beautiful he lost his breath. He couldn't speak, couldn't breathe. Couldn't do anything but stare at her. Her pale skin, her perfect breasts, the flat stomach and her nest of blond curls at the juncture of her thighs. And the years fell away. That rainy day in the playhouse. The day they'd gone clamming together, got soaked and came back to her house. But not to this house, this house bursting with people and lights and noise. No, they'd gone to the playhouse...

"You are so beautiful," he said gruffly. "So damned beautiful. And I want you so much..." But he couldn't have her. Not then and not now. There were too many ghosts standing between them. Her parents, his parents, her grandfather, the whole town— "Good God, what am I doing?" He grabbed her robe from the floor and threw it over her shoulders. Just as he heard a baby cry.

She stuffed her arms into the sleeves and picked up her nightgown from the floor. They stood frozen while the baby's cries rose.

"I've got to do something," she whispered.

"No, you don't. Babies cry," he said.

"And throw up," she added. "And have colic. I know, but..."

"Didn't the parents come back?" he asked.

"Yes, but..." She turned abruptly and said, "I'll go make sure everything's okay."

He followed her up the stairs and by the time they reached the door of the master bedroom the cries had subsided.

"See what I told you?" he said under his breath.

She nodded. "Goodnight, Sam," she whispered. Her eyes were burning bright in the pale nightlight. She reached up and brushed his lips with hers, then she went into her room. He didn't let himself respond. Didn't let himself pick her up and carry her into his room and make love to her all night. Because it wasn't meant to be. She knew it, he knew it. That kiss she gave him said it all. It was casual and affectionate. No passion there. As if they were old friends. Nothing more. Obviously she felt nothing for him except compassion. Which he could live without. He could also live without love and affection. It was obvious Hayley was glad he'd stopped when he had. What had happened down there in the kitchen was an example of lust out of control.

He stood staring at the closed door for a long time before he walked to his room, took off his wet clothes and went into the white-and-black-tiled bathroom with the stacks of fresh towels and soap redolent of fresh lavender. He opened the glass door and turned on the shower. Not a cold shower, which he badly needed, but a hot shower which he needed even more. The hot water stung his back and shoulders as he realized that only one day back in New Hope and he'd learned he was still lusting after the most beautiful girl in town, who had become the most beautiful woman, not just in New Hope, but anywhere.

And he'd learned he was still afraid of his father's ghost. Just two things he had to get over. He hadn't made progress on either front yet. But tomorrow was another day. He would try again.

Before he came to in the morning there were the smells. Creeping in under the door and filling the air. Of coffee and muffins and scones. All the things she'd promised. All the reasons to stay at a bed and breakfast. All the reasons to stay away from a woman you couldn't have. Waking up in a home with a woman in the kitchen making breakfast. Something he'd never missed because he'd never had it. Waking up to an incomparable view of the ocean outside his window and to the roar of the ocean, the sound of the waves crashing against the rocks a quarter of a mile away. More reasons to stay at the Bancroft House. The inn ought to be filled every night.

He looked at the old ship's clock on the bedside table and was shocked to find it was eight o'clock. He was normally in the OR by six. He never drank at night or slept late. How would he ever get back to normal after a six-month stay at the Bancroft House? How would he go back to a stark, sophisticated condo on Russian Hill that was more like a hotel than a home?

"I have to tell you," he said, sitting in the same seat at the breakfast bar, unable to tear his gaze from the curve of Hayley's hip as she bent over to lift pans out of the oven, palms itching to grab her around the waist and wrap his arms around her and bury his face in her hair. "I can't stay here for six months."

She set the muffins on the counter. Her face was flushed from the heat of the oven, and her hair was pinned back behind her ears. "Why not?"

"Isn't it obvious?"

She blushed, her face turning a deeper shade of scarlet.

"Drinking hot toddies at night and hot scones and lattes in the morning? I won't be able to fit into my scrubs."

"Oh, that," she said with relief.

"What did you think I was going to say?" he asked with a half smile.

"Nothing."

"Seriously, I can't impose on you this way," he said.

"It's not an imposition. It's my contribution to the community. Naturally if you were to stay on beyond the six months…"

"I won't be," he said curtly.

"You'd have to get a house of your own," she said as

if she hadn't heard him. "That's no problem. There are several for rent or for sale. And the community would be glad to—"

"I said I won't be," he repeated, reaching for a blueberry muffin and slathering it with sweet butter.

"Then there's no problem. I'm committed to providing bed and breakfast for the temporary doctor."

"You did that before you knew it was going to be me."

"It doesn't matter who it is. A guest is a guest."

He shrugged. Secretly relieved. He didn't want to leave this house. This house that she'd changed from a cold, elegant showpiece into a warm and welcoming home. He didn't want to give up seeing her at night and in the morning. "All right, but no more dinners."

She wiped her hands on her apron. "Okay," she said. She sounded hurt. Dammit. He'd hurt her feelings. When all he wanted to do was avoid falling into a routine that was going to be awkward to break.

"I already owe you for last night. And I always pay my debts, as you know," he said. "So tonight I take you to dinner."

"And then will we be even?" she asked.

"Yes. Is it a deal? Or are you busy?"

She wrinkled her nose and glanced at her computer on the counter, keyed in the week's calendar and shook her head. From what he could see there were a lot of empty spaces on the screen. "So far I'm free, but really…"

"Good." He drained his coffee cup. "What am I supposed to do now? Amble over to the office and see if anyone comes in?"

"I guess so," she said. "I've put out the word you're here, you may be swamped."

"I'll give out my cell phone number, then if there are

any emergencies..." he said. "I have my beeper. They can reach me any time."

"You'd do that?" she asked.

"That's what I'm here for."

"You may have to give up any private life," she said.

"I don't have one."

Hayley stood on the front steps, apron still tied around her waist, watching him walk down the long driveway to the street. He'd obviously chosen to walk the mile and a half to the office in an effort to burn off the three muffins he'd eaten for breakfast. As if Sam had an ounce of fat on his lean, muscular body.

The talk of him returning to San Francisco gave her a jolt, though she knew perfectly well that was the plan. She knew she shouldn't get attached to him, but she'd gotten attached to Sam years ago, and living under the same roof with him wasn't going to help her detach herself.

Still, she wouldn't give it up for anything. She loved seeing him first thing in the morning with his hair damp from the shower, even the lines around his mouth seemed to have relaxed. It was good for him to be back in New Hope. Despite the bad memories. He could make new memories, if he tried. Memories to take back to San Francisco. Because he would go. She had to keep telling herself that. There was nothing she could do to keep him there. She was sure he was counting the days.

And she had to prepare herself mentally for his leaving. As she ripped off the sheets in the master bedroom she reminded herself she should treat him like any other guest. No more late-night drinks, no kisses in the hall or the kitchen or anywhere. If she continued where they'd left off last night she'd be in worse shape than she'd been seventeen years ago when he'd left. Then she'd been young and foolish. Now she was old and sensible. But she hadn't felt sensible last night. She'd felt giddy and reckless. The last time Sam left, she'd been shipped off to college. This time she was staying here. There'd be no one to pick up the pieces when she fell apart.

She pushed the vacuum cleaner around the living room, muttering to herself that it would do no good to try to persuade Sam to stay on in New Hope. He didn't belong there. He was bored there. The most she could hope for, and it was a lot, was that he would come to terms with the town and his family and with her, of course. That he would leave a happier and calmer man than when he came, at peace with himself. If she could contribute to his improved state of mind, then she'd be happy too.

They still hadn't discussed the circumstances of his leaving town seventeen years ago. It was like a ticking time bomb. If Sam didn't bring it up, then she would. Otherwise it would always be there between them like a permanent wedge. Although she knew what she was going to say, she wasn't ready to say it. Not yet. Even if she'd been practicing for seventeen years. She needed to get her raging hormones under control. So she wouldn't be swayed by her feelings for him. Feelings that seemed just as strong as they were so long ago. Maybe stronger.

She willed the phone to ring. She wished for someone to call and make a reservation. Then she wouldn't have to go to dinner with Sam. She didn't want to go out with him. It was too hard to pretend indifference to him, to pretend he wasn't the sexiest man she'd ever known. And to pretend that she hadn't been in love with him half of her life. If he looked carefully, and he had a way of looking at her very carefully, he was going to see the feelings she was hiding. At home there was always someplace to hide. But in his car or in a restaurant...where was she going to hide?

She finished her housework and drove to the office at noon. Just in time to see a grizzled old man in baggy coveralls with a very pregnant young woman, neither of whom she'd ever seen before, standing at the front door, talking to Mattie. Hayley stood on the sidewalk, shamelessly listening to their conversation and staring at the woman with her long, stringy hair, her denim jacket unbuttoned over her bulging stomach and her dusty shoes.

"Doctor Bancroft isn't with us any more," Mattie explained stiffly. "Doctor Prentice is filling in temporarily."

"Never heard of him," the man said.

"Sam Prentice. From right here in New Hope," Mattie said.

"Cal Prentice's son?" the man asked incredulously.

"That's the one. He's a doctor now. Would your daughter like to see him today? I can make an appointment for you."

The man grabbed his daughter by the arm and dragged her down the steps. "You kiddin' me? Let that kid touch my daughter? That'll be the day. He's got a hell of a nerve coming back here. After what his pa did."

Hayley's stomach twisted into knots. She hoped Sam couldn't hear him. But he had heard him.

"What was that all about?" she asked, when she found him standing in the waiting room, looking out the open window watching the pair walk slowly down Main Street. Mattie was standing there, too, her gray cardigan sweater buttoned up and her handbag over her shoulder as if she was ready to leave, but not before she told her side of the story.

"You don't want to know," Sam said with a dour expression.

"Yes, I do," she insisted.

"There are some things I can't tell you," he said.

"Can't or won't?" she asked.

His eyes flashed. "What about the things you can't or won't tell me?"

She stiffened. Not now. Not in front of Mattie. "All right," she said. "That's fair. But not now."

"I've heard that before. 'Not now.' When?"

"Later."

"Tonight," he said.

She glanced at Mattie. Mattie shifted her curious gaze from Hayley to Sam and back again.

"Who were those people?" Hayley asked, glancing out the window. "I didn't recognize them."

"Their name's Harris. Ignorant people," Mattie said. "Girl got herself knocked up and the father wants her to see your grandfather. Nobody else. Like Doc Bancroft was waiting around to deliver her baby. She'll be lucky to find anybody to do it."

"They sure don't want me," Sam said. "Something to do with my father. The man's been gone for twenty-some years, but his memory lingers on," he said, scowling.

Hayley knew he was talking about his own memories of his father, as well. She resisted the urge to smooth the lines in his forehead. To tell him to let it go. It wouldn't do any good.

Mattie muttered something under her breath that sounded like "Could have told you." Then she straightened her shoulders and said, "It's their loss. Now, if you all will excuse me." Before she walked out the door, she turned to Hayley. "Believe it or not, he's got some appointments this afternoon. They're in the book there." Then she closed the door behind her.

"Did I hear right? Did Mattie just say 'it's their loss'?" Hayley asked.

"I heard her say 'told you.'"

"Nevertheless, you must have impressed her."

"I doubt it. She spent the morning telling me how I'd never be as good as your grandfather, as if that was my goal. 'Doctor Bancroft always made house calls. Everyone always loved Doctor Bancroft.' Well, I've never made a house call in my life. I wouldn't mind making them, but I don't expect to be loved. That's not what I'm here for."

Hayley could see by the bleak look in his eyes and his clipped tones that this was true. He didn't expect to be loved, because he never was. Except by her. Was she the only one who'd ever loved him? Still loved him? She wanted to throw her arms around him and tell him, but she couldn't. She could only imagine what he'd say. That her imagination was running overtime. That she was an incurable romantic. That she should grow up. That love didn't exist except for dreamers.

She ached for him. Deep in her soul. She wanted to make it right. Erase the years of neglect. Erase the past and undo what the past had done to him. But she couldn't. He wouldn't let her even try.

Instead of telling him he was lovable, she said, "I brought you some lunch," and set a basket on Mattie's desk.

"I don't eat lunch."

"But you should. I always used to bring something for Grandpa. He always said nobody made meat loaf sandwiches like mine. He said that's what kept him going. So I thought—"

"Grandpa always said this. Doc Bancroft always did that. No wonder you can't get anyone to take this job. Nobody could ever compete with him," Sam said bitterly. "I've been getting along without someone making my meals for twenty years or more. I think I can make it through the next six months."

"What about Marion, your guard dog. Didn't she ever bring you a sandwich for lunch?" she asked.

"That's different," he said. "I pay her a good salary. I'm not paying you anything. Or am I?" he asked.

"No, of course not. I'm a volunteer." She had pictured them sharing lunch in the back room or maybe even the park, but that was not going to happen. Sam was not the kind of man to take time out, even though he had nothing to do. It had gotten to be a habit, she realized. Work, work and more work. Because if he stopped he would fall behind. Someone else would take his place, and he'd be back in the gutter where he came from.

"What have you been doing?" she asked, afraid he'd say there was nothing to do.

"Some research for a paper I'm writing on early intervention in myocardial infarctions. I'm giving it at a symposium next month in Seattle. That is if I can get away." His gaze swept over the empty office and she managed a weak smile. It was his way of telling her he was not needed. That she'd exaggerated the whole problem of the town without a doctor.

"If you don't mind, I'll run over to the newspaper office, then," she said. "And check on my ad."

"While you're out I need a few things from the pharmacy. There is a pharmacy, isn't there?"

"Scotty's Drugstore. They don't have everything, but—"

"Cotton swabs? Rubbing alcohol? Tongue depressants?"

She nodded. "I'll see what I can do."

He reached in his pocket and pulled out a wad of bills.

"No, no, I'll get it."

"Take it," he said grimly. He opened her palm, pressed the money into it and folded her fingers around it.

"When I get back we'll put in a large order," she promised.

"Sure you want to do that?" he asked. Again a reference to the lack of patients.

"Yes, sure." She had to act confident; if she didn't he would leave. "It's just the first day."

"Yeah," Sam said with a glance at the calendar on the wall. "Just the first day."

From the window he watched Hayley walk down the street, shoulders back, head held high, her arms swinging confidently at her sides. Did she ever have any doubt that she'd succeed? He didn't think so. She had faith in her business, faith in her town and faith in him—even years ago when he hadn't deserved it. She was much too good for this town. She ought to be somewhere where she'd be appreciated, compensated for her talents. Here she was struggling to make ends meet. Baby-sitting and baking muffins. That was her parents' fault. Bringing her up to want for nothing, then throwing their money into the stock market and leaving her with nothing but the house. A big expensive house at that.

He went back to his computer, but on the way he spotted the picnic basket on the desk. She meant well, bringing him his lunch, but he didn't want her to take care of him. Didn't want to depend on her. On the other hand, he didn't want the food to go to waste. So he took out a sandwich, some potato salad and a thermos of coffee and went back to the lab. He ate, but he couldn't concentrate on his research. He kept thinking about Hayley. Remembering how she looked in her nightgown last night. The sight of her pale breasts so tantalizing, the curve of her stomach, her hips, the smell of her skin. If that baby hadn't cried, what would have happened? He wanted to make love to her, not the clumsy way they'd almost done it as randy teenagers, but as mature adults—mature adults who had unfinished business between them. His heart rate sped up just thinking about his lost opportunity last night.

How far was she willing to go with him? How far was he willing to go with her before he had to tell her there was no future for them? Hell, she knew that. She knew that better than anyone. He wouldn't even have to explain it. He didn't believe in love or marriage. The reasons were obvious. He'd been a loner all his life. First out of necessity, then out of choice.

But she was special. The only person in the world who'd known him then and now. He steered clear of relationships, of messy entanglements. But this wouldn't need to be messy. It would have a beginning and an end. The beginning would be tonight. The end would be in six months. She appeared to like him. God knew why, with his temperament. And was still attracted to him, if last night was any indication.

As for him, he was attracted to her, even more than he'd been when he was a lust-filled teenager. He thought about her; he couldn't stop. He fantasized about making love to her. He didn't want to stop fantasizing. It was harmless, or was it? She'd metamorphosed from a pretty, spoiled rich girl with a weakness for the town bad boy into a beautiful, sensitive, capable woman with a weakness for kids and her town and for him, too. At least he thought so. He had to find out.

Six

A few minutes later the bell over the door rang, and he went to the front office to see a young boy standing there, black eye, bloody nose, dirty shirt and torn pants.

"Where's the doctor?" the boy asked.

"I'm the doctor," Sam said.

"Where's the old guy?"

"He died. What happened to you?" Sam asked, putting his hand on the boy's shoulder and leading him into the examining room.

"Got in a fight," he said.

"Uh-huh." Sam took his dirty shirt off, then his ripped pants, cleaned him up and did a quick checkup before he bandaged his cuts. He didn't wince or complain. Sam admired that.

"How old are you?"

"Twelve and a half."

"Who started it?"

"They did. They said I was a... They called me names," the kid said, his lip swollen and his mouth twisted into a frown. Sam nodded. It all came back to him. The insults.

Your mother's a whore.

Your pa's a drunk.

Trailer trash.

The schoolyard fights. Only he'd never had the nerve to walk into the doctor's office like that. It was Hayley who'd brought him in, more than once. Dragged him in. Under duress. It was her grandfather who'd patched him up. Who'd asked him the same questions he was asking now.

"Where're your parents?"

"My mom's at work."

The way he shifted his gaze told Sam the kid was lying. Just as he himself might have lied to Doc Bancroft. Maybe the boy's mother was passed out on the couch after a night in the bar, or maybe she'd taken off, leaving him alone in a travel trailer on the edge of town. Both scenarios were familiar to Sam.

"Have her call me," he said, handing the dirty shirt back to the boy.

"Why?" he asked, struggling into his jeans. "She ain't got no money to pay you."

"That's okay. I just want to tell her to change your bandages," Sam said, handing him a tube of disinfectant and a package of bandages.

"I can do it myself."

"Sure you can," Sam said. Sam patted him on the back even though he knew it embarrassed him. It was just an impulse. One he instantly regretted when he saw the boy's eyes widen in alarm. "What's your name?" Sam asked.

"Roy."

"Don't fight anymore, Roy," he said. Oh, that was helpful. That ought to do it. "Come back and see me next week. I need to check you out."

"I can't pay you."

"Doesn't matter."

The boy gave him a long, level look out of sad, dark eyes. And he knew if he ever had a son, he'd teach him to defend himself. He'd give him no reason to be picked on, to be called names. Though this kid hadn't done too badly, it seemed.

"Hey," Sam said as the kid turned to leave. "You like meat loaf sandwiches?"

Roy shrugged, and Sam opened the basket and pulled one neatly wrapped sandwich out and gave it to him. He unwrapped it and looked at it suspiciously. Then he smelled it. Sam stifled a smile.

"Go ahead, it won't poison you," Sam said.

"You make it?"

"Me? No, I can't cook," Sam said. "A friend of mine made it."

The boy took a bite and chewed hungrily. Sam knew what it was like to feel the gnawing pangs of hunger. He wondered when the boy had eaten last. He looked too thin under his faded cotton shirt.

"Thanks," Roy said, and he was gone as suddenly as he'd arrived. Before Sam could even ask where he lived.

When Hayley came back Sam said, "You missed all the excitement. I had a patient." When he told her who it was, she shook her head.

"I used to know everyone in town," she said. "Not anymore. I'm worried about him. No mother?"

"Don't worry. He can take care of himself."

"The way you did?" she asked. She unpacked the supplies and put them on the shelves of the cabinet.

"You do what you have to do," he said, and sat down to face his computer, hoping to end the conversation.

"Did you have to run away that last night?" she asked.

He felt the heat of anger rush through his body. He stared at the screen without seeing it. "You know the answer to that. I had to 'run away' as you put it, because the sheriff came looking for me." The memories came charging back, the flashing lights on the sheriff's car, running down the back streets to the highway, his head pounding from his injuries, catching a ride from a trucker to Portland with only the clothes on his back.

"You blame Grandpa for that, don't you?"

"Who else would have reported me?" he asked.

"Don't you understand?" she asked. "He had to. As a doctor you know the rules."

"There are times when you have to bend the rules," he said coldly. He'd never forgive them for what they did. She and her grandfather had robbed him of a chance to defend himself, the opportunity to graduate with his class and his reputation. Not that his reputation was much to speak of to begin with, but running was never his style. And they'd forced him to run.

"He bent the rules for you more than once," she said, "but that time—"

"That time he thought I was to blame. He thought I'd started the fight. So did you, didn't you? When it counted I couldn't trust you."

"Sam…"

He turned to face her. She was leaning against the wall and gnawing on her lower lip. Her eyes were glistening. "Don't cry for me, Hayley. It's a little late for that."

"I—I'm not."

"Just forget it," he ordered. "It was seventeen years ago. Everything turned out fine in the long run. I'd forgotten all about it. Until you walked into my office and reminded me.''

"I'm sorry, but I think we need to talk about it, otherwise..."

"Otherwise what? We don't need to talk about it. We just did talk about it. We don't need to talk any further. Your grandfather regretted what he'd done. He must have or he wouldn't have paid my way through school. I'm here to repay my debt. Then we'll be even and we can go on with our lives. Is that a deal?'' he asked.

She nodded, but he knew he hadn't heard the last of it. She wanted to talk it out. To rehash the whole episode. Over and over. But he was not going to be a party to that kind of pointless recrimination. He turned to his computer, stared at the screen until she got the hint and went out to the waiting room to wait for patients.

That evening at five she closed and locked the office after he'd seen a handful of patients with minor complaints. As he'd told Hayley, they didn't need a high-priced surgeon. Anyone with a shred of common sense could have dealt with their problems. Mattie, for example. But that wasn't the way it worked. Patients wanted to know they were in the hands of an M.D. They wanted to see his diploma on the wall. So he hung it there. And stared at it. And waited.

He felt useless and bored. He was used to a frantic pace. Of having his beeper going off constantly. Of performing surgery and making rounds and lecturing med students.

Hayley offered him a ride home, but he declined. He was already regretting that he'd asked her to dinner. So, no doubt, was she. Spending time together was not wise. He'd told her it wasn't going to work, his returning to New Hope, living and working with her. He was right. He'd only asked her to dinner as a courtesy. He owed her dinner and he was going to take her to dinner.

She met him at the big oak door with Bancroft House carved into a thick cedar shingle that hung over the door from loops of wrought-iron. His gaze traveled over her faded jeans and pullover. Dressed like that, her hair pulled back from her face with a barrette, she looked so much the way she'd looked in high school. A heart-stopping combination of innocence and sensuality he hadn't been able to resist then or now. And yet she was not the same at all. She had a smooth grace about her now, a quiet confidence that said she was not a woman to trifle with. She was a woman who would not settle for anything but the best. Who in the hell had she married? Why wasn't she still married?

He clenched his hands into fists to keep from grabbing her and kissing her. To shake her up. To make her admit she'd missed him. That every time she'd made love over the past seventeen years, she'd thought of him as he'd thought of her. Hah. Not likely. Why else would she have married someone else? It didn't last, but she must have loved the guy. Damn her for loving someone else. She'd once told him she would never love anyone but him. She wouldn't remember that.

And damn her calm, cool demeanor. He glanced up at the wide staircase, half expecting to hear her mother's voice calling down the stairs as she'd once done when he had the nerve to come to the front door. Hayley, who is it? Who's at the door? It's not that boy, is it? Close the door. Get rid of him. It *is* him, isn't it? The one from the wrong side of town. The one who's always in trouble.

''I thought we'd go to that seafood restaurant in New-port if it's still there,'' he said, jerking himself back to the present after the silence had lasted entirely too long for comfort.

"Oh, I can't. I just got a call. I've got a couple coming in from Portland. I want to be here when they arrive. I'm sorry. Some other time?" she suggested. But she didn't look sorry. She looked relieved. And what if she was making it up to avoid having dinner with him?

"Of course," he said tersely. It was a bad idea, anyway, spending any more time with her than necessary. Already it was going to be every afternoon. But he didn't feel relieved, not the way she did. He felt let down. He hadn't realized how much he'd looked forward to spending time with her, spending money on her, too, showing her just how far he'd come, how much he'd changed. But that was ridiculous. And immaterial. She knew he'd changed. It didn't matter.

So he turned around, got into his car and drove to Newport, anyway, ate at the expensive restaurant overlooking the harbor, overtipped the waitress, then walked around endlessly, looking at the tourists, killing time. Of all the ironies—he, who'd never had enough time for himself since he'd worked his way through college and gone to medical school, now found himself having way too much time on his hands.

Finally, after an appropriate amount of time elapsed, an agonizingly slow amount of time, during which he strode up and down the streets looking into store windows that contained totally useless items that would appeal only to tourists, he drove back to Bancroft House. There was a new BMW parked in front of the house. So she really had guests. He'd had more than one moment of doubt that she was really expecting anyone. During the evening he became convinced she'd made the reservation up to avoid his company. He stared up at her darkened bedroom window, thought about throwing a stone at it, imagined her opening the window, watching her nightgown swirl around her...but not tonight. Tonight he had no excuse. She'd provided him with his own key. But he continued to stand there, willing her to turn on her light, to come to the window and see him there. But she didn't, so he finally took out his key and let himself in.

The lights were dim in the living room. A crystal decanter of sherry was on the mantel, warm embers still in the fireplace. Maybe she'd spent the evening with the guests, advising them of the local attractions, amusing them with anecdotes and local history. He was filled with an unaccountable envy for these unknown guests.

What in the hell was wrong with him, envying some damned faceless tourists? And how on earth would he ever make it through the next six months?

The next day there was more of the same. A brief breakfast with Hayley. Morning in the office with Mattie. Afternoon in the office with Hayley at the desk in the front office. A few patients with minor complaints. In between patients he tried working on his paper, but he kept tilting back in his chair, looking out the window, listening for Hayley's voice, wanting to walk down the hall to her desk and talk to her, tease her, flirt with her. Hear her laugh, watch her blush and listen to her talk. But he couldn't do that. He was here to be the doctor. He was a grown man now. A doctor. He could have any woman he wanted. Except for her.

She represented everything he'd ever wanted and couldn't have: beauty, class, money and prestige. Now he could have those things, but he couldn't have her. She was still out of his league. No matter how much money he had, how esteemed he was as a doctor, she was still Hayley

Bancroft and he was still Sam Prentice. Coming back to New Hope had been a big mistake.

He didn't mention dinner to her again that week. And she didn't mention it to him. He ate at the diner every night, risking been recognized as the town bad boy, but it was better than driving into Newport. There was a warm, friendly atmosphere in the diner. Neighbors greeted each other, stopped by each other's table and chatted. No one noticed him. He was on the outside where he'd always been. No one stopped by his table, which was fine with him. He didn't need friends.

Hayley hadn't had any guests all week, as far as he could tell, so he was doubly proud of himself for not suggesting dinner. Until Saturday.

Saturday morning Sam sat down at the small breakfast table in Hayley's spacious kitchen and watched her make Belgian waffles. She was wearing jeans and a sweater with a huge white chef's apron tied around her waist. She had a smudge of sugar on her cheek that was driving him crazy. Along with the apron. He held his coffee cup in a tight grip to remind himself not to give in to temptation and move up behind her, untie her apron and pull her to him so close he could wrap his arms around her, her little bottom nestled in the apex of his thighs, his hands on the swell of her breasts. No matter what she wore, a robe or an apron, he found himself wanting to take it off. Imagining how she'd look without it. Without anything.

He wanted to lick the sugar off her cheek and kiss her until their lips stuck together, until the sugar melted—or forever, for that matter. But that wasn't going to happen. Nothing was going to happen as long as he had an ounce of self-preservation in his body. No way was he going to set himself up for another painful departure from New

Hope. This time he was walking out with no regrets, no ties, and no backward glance.

Which required him to stay cool. To keep his distance from Hayley, both emotional and physical. Which was why he'd postponed the dinner he'd promised her and turned down her offers for deep-sea fishing, kite flying or clamming. Because he was afraid she'd tag along, thinking he needed company. He didn't. He'd been on his own all his life, and while it wasn't the easiest way to grow up, it had become his way of life.

He drained his coffee cup and got up off the stool at the breakfast counter. He was going somewhere. He had to. He just didn't know where. The office was closed on Saturday, and the day stretched ahead of him, empty and pointless. Why hadn't he taken Al up on the cruise idea? It had sounded ludicrous at the time, but more and more it sounded like a better idea than returning to the town he'd forgotten and the girl he'd been trying to forget for seventeen years.

Rain pelted the windows, and the heat from the antique ceramic stove, coupled with the steam from the hot coffee, wrapped around him like a cocoon. Tighter and tighter until he couldn't breathe. He had to get out of there. Away from her and her house. It made him want things he'd never had and certainly never wanted. Home and hearth and a long weekend ahead of him and someone to share it with. To walk in the rain with, to return to bed with, to make love with, share his thoughts with, laugh with....

"Well, I'm off," he said, ending his traitorous thoughts as briskly as if he had someplace to go. Something to do. Someone to do it with. "I still owe you a dinner," he said nonchalantly. "We can go tonight, if you still want to." As if she would ever want to go. But he had to take her out. He owed her. He'd promised her.

"Of course," she said. So stiff, so polite. As if he were just another guest. As if they were strangers.... They might as well be for all the contact they'd had during the past week. She'd said yes, but he was convinced she would think up some reason to cancel again.

He drove up the coast, stopping at a beautiful, deserted beach strewn with bleached driftwood, changed into running shorts and shoes and ran for miles until his lungs were raw and empty, until he had to stop and gasp for breath, until his muscles hurt and his body begged for relief. Until he stopped thinking about Hayley. Until he finally turned around and drove back.

"Business *will* pick up for you," Hayley said, sitting across from him at their window table at the Sea Change restaurant. "As soon as word gets around." They hadn't talked much on the way to the restaurant. He hadn't been very forthcoming about what he'd done that day. He'd seemed surprised when she'd agreed to have dinner with him. When he walked back into the house, his grim expression told her he hadn't had the greatest time, whatever he'd been doing. Not that she expected him to rave about the simple pleasures of a day along the Oregon coast. Nor had she expected him to ask her along. She'd merely thought, merely imagined he might want company. He'd made it quite clear he didn't. Not hers, anyway.

Now she was determined to act normal. As if Sam were an old friend. No more. No less. He was right. There was no need to rehash the past. It was over.

"It doesn't matter," he said. "I'm here whether they need me or not."

"They need you," she insisted. "But in the meantime, what about doing some deep-sea fishing tomorrow?"

Which was just what she would have suggested to any guest.

"You don't have to entertain me. I'm not a guest," he said as if he'd read her mind.

"Well then, how about clamming?" she persisted.

He shrugged.

"Dammit, Sam, you're determined to have a miserable time for six months, aren't you?" she asked.

"I'd rather not waste my time, that's all."

"Is it wasting your time to relax, to take a well-deserved break? I thought that was the idea of your coming here." She would give anything to see those lines in his forehead relax, to see him smile, hear him laugh.

"My reason for coming here was to repay your grandfather. If it hadn't been for that—"

"You'd be on a Caribbean cruise, is that what you're saying?" she asked.

"I wonder. No, I don't think I'm the cruise type. Too restless. All right, I didn't have anything else to do. Does it make you happy to know you gave me a place to go?" he asked.

"It makes me happy to see you stop working eighty-hour weeks."

"That must surprise you, that I would work so hard at something."

She shook her head and took a sip of the expensive merlot he'd ordered. "Not at all. You were always... intense."

His mouth quirked up at one corner. It wasn't really a smile. It was too cynical. But it was a start. "Intense," he repeated, tapping his spoon on the table. "Don't you mean wild, offensive, delinquent, derelict...?"

"I meant intense and intelligent, intuitive and just plain smart. And I wasn't the only one who thought that."

"I know. That's why— Never mind."

"I know what you were going to say. That's why it hurt
so much when Grandpa turned you in. He believed in you.
He knew you had potential. That you could succeed." She
leaned forward and propped her elbows on the table.
"Would you believe me if I told you it hurt him more than
it hurt you?"

"Oh, right. I'm sure it did." His voice dripped with
sarcasm. "Let's forget about it. Put it behind us. It was
seventeen years ago. I got over it. He did, too. And so did
you."

If he only knew. She'd never gotten over it or over him.
She'd never found anyone like him. She sometimes wondered if that was why her marriage had turned out so dis-
astrously. Because she'd been looking for someone to take
his place. But no one could. No one had that combination
of intensity, intelligence and animal magnetism. No one
ever made her feel the way he did. Now was her chance
to forget it, put it behind her, as he so succinctly suggested.
Now was the time to take a good look at the boy who ran
away and at the man he'd become and close that chapter
of her life. She'd have plenty of time to do that. Six
months. Maybe too much time.

She glanced across the table. He was looking at her with
those jet-black eyes, his expression carefully neutral. Did
he ever let go? Did he ever really enjoy himself? Or had
he truly turned into a workaholic whose only pleasure was
work and more work? Granted, it was important work,
humanitarian work. But work all the same.

"You're right, of course," she said as the waiter grated
fresh Parmesan cheese over her Caesar salad. "The past
is the past. Here's to the future." She raised her glass.

He lifted his wineglass and tapped hers. "Yours or
mine?" he asked.

"Both. What do you see in your future, Sam? More o
the same?"

He set his glass down, musing. "I could be chief o
staff one day. Then they might name a wing of the hospita
after me. Or at least a plaque in the lobby. I could go into
research. Invent a new heart valve. Leave something be
hind me when I die. And I'd have more regular hours tha
way. More time off."

"Time for golf?" she asked.

"No golf," he said.

"What, then, if you refuse to go fishing—wine, wome
and song?"

"I always have time for women, as long as they don'
interfere with my job," he said.

"You mean as long as they don't count on you to shov
up for some prearranged appointment—like Christma:
birthdays, weddings and funerals? No wonder you neve
got married."

"That's not why I never got married," he said, his gaz
fastened on the view of the harbor lights.

"No?" she asked lightly, hoping she didn't sound to
interested.

"No," he said firmly. And she knew that was all sh
was going to get out of him that night. "Speaking of mar
riage," he said as the waiter set a plate of crab cakes wit
remoulade sauce in front of each of them. "What hap
pened to yours?"

She winced at his blunt question, then gathered her com
posure like a jacket around her. "Oh, just the usual. Irred
oncilable differences. Incompatibility."

"What was the matter, he didn't like your making blue
berry muffins for anybody but him?" he asked.

"No, that wasn't it. It was before I had the bed an

breakfast. Before I had the confidence to be my own person, before I knew what I wanted from life.''

''And what's that?'' he asked

''Peace. Tranquillity.''

''Maybe your life's a little too tranquil,'' he suggested, cutting into his crisp, savory crab cake. ''Maybe it's time you shook it up a little.''

''Really. What do you suggest?'' she asked.

''Take a motorcycle ride. Go back to Africa. Take a safari.''

''You should talk. According to your boss you work too hard and you never take vacations. And you have no excuse. You have six months off. And the money to do what you want.'' She set her fork down. ''I'm sorry,'' she said contritely. ''If it weren't for me interfering in your life, that's exactly what you would be doing. *Could* be doing.''

''It's always easier to tell someone else what's wrong with their lives, isn't it?'' he asked. ''Like 'You need to take a break. Take time off. Go on vacation. Get married. Play golf.'''

''Or ride a motorcycle,'' she murmured. ''You don't still have a motorcycle, do you?'' she asked.

''As a matter of fact I just bought myself a new street bike. If I had it here, I'd take you for a ride.''

''I remember the last time you took me for a ride. We were stopped for speeding by Officer Spaulding. My parents found out and I was grounded for two weeks.'' But that's not the part she remembered most. The part she'd never forget was how it felt to be plastered against his back, the throbbing of the engine, the wind in her hair, the freedom, the exhilaration.

''I was a bad influence on you,'' he said with a cocky grin that made him look like the teenage, daredevil Sam. Made her return his smile. Made her realize that under-

neath that successful doctor façade, a trace of the town bad
boy still lurked. Much more than a trace. The years had
been good to him; no doubt about it. Financial success had
smoothed off some of the rough edges, given him self-
assurance, but underneath was a raw energy and ambition
that attracted her with the power of a supermagnet. She
couldn't take her eyes off him. Couldn't stop wishing for
another ride on his motorcycle. Another chance to press
her body against his.

"And you're not a bit sorry for it," she said with a half
smile.

"Why should I be? You were a goody-goody. Your parents' obedient daughter. What I want to know is, are you
still?" he asked, his eyes narrowed, his voice low.

"My parents' daughter? No, of course not," she said
"I'm my own person now. I grew up."

"Yes, I can see that," he said, leaning back in his chair
his bold gaze skimming the outline of her breasts under
her sweater. Reminding her of that day in the playhouse
when she'd peeled her wet sweater off, then her bra and
flung them on the floor. Remembering his cool hands on
her feverish skin.

"And so did you," she said, shifting uncomfortably as
her face flushed, a shiver ran up her spine and her nipples
tightened under her sweater. Hoping he wouldn't notice in
the subdued light, hoping he'd long ago forgotten the in-
cident that shook her world. That afternoon, that moment
when they'd almost... She'd nearly... So long ago, and
yet, just yesterday. "We both grew up," she said.

"I don't hot-wire cars anymore, if that's what you mean
But underneath I'm basically the same hotshot kid, out to
show the world I'm as good as the next person. Isn't that
what you thought of me?" he asked.

"Well..." I thought you were the most exciting person

I'd ever known. The sexiest, the most daring, the most provocative... She took a sip of ice water and cleared her throat.

"Never mind," he said brusquely. "I know what you thought of me. You haven't told me who you married."

"No one you know."

"Where did you meet him?"

"In Portland."

She didn't intend to say any more, but he just sat there, looking at her, waiting for her to continue, so at last she did.

"It was after I got out of the Peace Corps. I was at loose ends. Wanting to change the world, but not knowing how to go about it. So I joined this save-the-trees group. He was an active environmentalist—save the trees, the birds, the frogs, whatever species needed saving." Except for one. "We had protests, chained ourselves to the redwoods," she said lightly as if it had all been a game. But it hadn't been. It had been deadly serious. She paused while the waiter brought coffee and a chocolate decadence. Just time enough to regret pouring out her life story.

Nobody wanted to hear the details of that stage of her life. Not her parents, who'd actively opposed her marriage to an offbeat do-gooder, and not her friends who'd never understood what she saw in him. And especially not Sam. Though he'd just prodded her to tell him who she'd married. *Who,* she reminded herself, not how and why.

"You don't want to hear all this," she said. "I don't know why I'm going on about it."

"I asked," he said.

"I...you asked where I met him. The answer is Portland."

"You can't stop now. Not in the middle of the story. Not when you've just chained yourself to a redwood. Then what? Did the lumber company cut your tree down on top of you or were you arrested?''

She shook her head. ''Neither. Nothing so dramatic. I got cold and tired and unchained myself and went home. But he didn't.''

''He?''

''Todd, my husband, but he wasn't my husband yet. He was tough and tenacious and idealistic.'' Hayley didn't say that he was also coldly disappointed in her. She glanced at Sam. His expression was unreadable. ''I think you've heard enough,'' she said.

''Not yet. Go on. Continue. Did you love him?'' he asked, his mouth set in a straight line.

She ran her finger around the rim of her empty wineglass. ''I don't know. I know I admired him. And I wanted to be like him. Wanted to have clear-cut goals like his. But...'' She trailed off, knowing she was skirting dangerous territory, knowing she had to wrap it up quickly before she got into the bad part, the part that tore her apart even now, so many years later. ''But as it turned out, our goals were quite different. So we got a divorce.'' She was proud of how calm and casual she sounded. When inside the wound still festered. The pain lingered. Would always be there.

''That's it? Why do I get the feeling there's something missing?'' he asked.

Because there *was* something missing. Something that hurt so badly to think about, she was certainly not going to speak about it. Ever. Not to anyone. Especially not to Sam, who'd always had a sixth sense about those things. An ability to see beneath the surface. To read between the lines. Which probably had served him well as a doctor.

She was saved from answering when she spotted her friends Pete and Donna Lamb in the restaurant. She might have only smiled at them across the room. But, given the circumstances, the fact that Sam was looking at her expectantly, waiting for her to continue with a story she didn't want to tell, she waved at them and beckoned them to their table.

Sam turned and stiffened when he saw them. Hayley didn't know what kind of history he'd had with them, but his scowl indicated it wasn't a pleasant one. Nevertheless he stood and smiled politely when they reached the table. Someone along the line must have taught him manners, Hayley thought, and wondered who and when. Maybe it was a class in bedside manners at medical school.

"Donna, you remember Sam Prentice, don't you?" she asked. "Sam's taking over Grandpa's medical office for a few months."

"Hi, Sam. Welcome back. You probably don't remember me," Donna said with a smile while Pete shook his hand.

"Yes, I do. You were a cheerleader." He remembered her only too well. One of the popular girls in Hayley's tight, little crowd. Her husband had been on the football team. Sam fought off a strong inclination to dislike them both as much as he'd envied them so many years ago. Envied the security of their decent homes, parents who cared, money to buy food and clothes. He told himself things had changed. Donna didn't act or look snobbish the way he remembered. And Pete seemed like a nice enough guy who'd put on a few pounds since his varsity days.

"Won't you join us?" he asked.

"We're just leaving," Donna said. "I just wanted to say hello."

"Low tide tomorrow at 7:00 a.m.," Pete said. "You two up for some serious digging and eating? Bet you haven't had anything like an Esperanza Bay clam since you left New Hope, Sam.''

''It's been a while,'' he said, shooting Hayley a suspicious look. Was it coincidence that everyone was trying to get him out digging clams? The truth was he'd never tasted a clam fresh out of the bay. He'd dug clams all right, but instead of rushing home to steam them in white wine and garlic, the way other beachcombers did, he'd sold them to the cook shack at the pier to make money. He'd had clams since then, at the finest restaurants, steamed and stuffed, in soups and salads, but never in his hometown.

''So what do you say?'' Pete asked, his gaze moving from Sam to Hayley.

''Count me in,'' Hayley said. ''I've got a new recipe for chowder I want to try.''

Three heads swiveled in Sam's direction, waiting for him to say something. He thought of spending another day by himself and decided it wouldn't hurt to spend it with Hayley and her friends. As long as it wasn't just the two of them, things shouldn't get too intense. On the other hand, he was more curious than ever about her life during the past seventeen years. She hadn't said it, but he felt sure there was more to her divorce than ''irreconcilable differences.'' Her normally open expression had closed when he tried to find out more.

Sam had learned not to accept a patient's story at face value. Often there were symptoms they were hiding, for one reason or another. Shame or fear or failure to pay attention. He was especially good at ferreting out deep-seated causes for physical problems. There had been a time when he was tempted to do a rotation in psychiatry, but he preferred surgery, enjoyed the team spirit in the OR, the ability to perform miracles with his hands and his equipment. It was just when things went wrong, when he couldn't perform the miracle that he wondered if he'd made the right decision.

Hayley was hiding something from him. He didn't know why and he didn't know what. But he'd find out sooner or later. He would get to the bottom of it, by spending more time with her and prodding her until she finally came out with the whole story.

"Why not?" he said at last, when he realized they were waiting for him to make up his mind.

They made plans to meet at the beach the next morning. Donna and Pete said good-night, and Sam asked for the check.

"Just out of curiosity, am I being set up to do the New Hope thing?" he asked.

She smiled. "I swear it was a coincidence. It's just that it's clamming season. If you don't want to go, don't."

"I'll go," he said, just as his beeper went off. He stared at it for a long moment as if he'd forgotten what to do. It had only been a little more than a week and already he was out of the loop.

"Who in the hell could that be?" he asked, showing Hayley the number of the caller on the screen.

Hayley's eyes widened. "It's Mattie."

Sam took his cell phone from his pocket and called her number.

"Sam, that horrible old man called the office and left a message," Mattie said. "Harris, is his name, the one who didn't want you to lay a hand on his precious daughter, Shawnee."

"Yeah, I remember them," he said.

"Well it seems she's in labor, yelling and screaming in pain. He's worried. He's changed his attitude about you, I can tell you. He's begging you to come out there. Shall I tell him you're too busy?" she asked.

"Out where?" he asked.

"By the dump on the Old Mill Road."

"The dump," Sam repeated. "I know where that is." Hadn't he spent hours pawing through the garbage looking for one thing or another? Something he could use or something he could sell. "We'll be there in an hour."

"We? Is Hayley with you?" Mattie asked, surprise and disapproval in her voice. "Where are you two? I tried the house. Nobody answered."

"We're having dinner in Newport," he said. Not that it was any of her business.

"Humph. I thought—never mind."

"You can call them back and tell them we're on our way," he said.

"Both of you?" Mattie asked.

"I'll need help. Unless you'd like to come along, Mattie. I'll swing by for you."

"No, sir," she said indignantly. "You wouldn't catch me down that road at this time of night. Not with that trash. Besides I don't do babies. Doc Bancroft always—"

"I know. Doc Bancroft always grabbed his little black bag and rode off into the sunset, solo, delivering perfect babies who were all named after him. But I'm a surgeon. I don't do babies, either. Except tonight I do. And I need all the help I can get. That's why I'm taking Hayley. And my computer and some equipment. Tell them we'll be there as soon as we can, would you?"

"If you say so, but you're under no obligation to these people, you know. They weren't Doc Bancroft's patients."

"Who is their doctor?" he asked.

"Hah. Far as I can tell, that girl has never seen anybody. That old man wouldn't trust anyone, even if there had been a doctor in town."

Sam paid the check while he kept the phone wedged

between his chin and his shoulder. Mattie continued to expound in his ear, as he and Hayley left the restaurant, about how these people didn't deserve his help after what they'd said about him.

When she finally hung up they were on the road speeding back to New Hope.

"I hope you don't mind coming along," Sam said. "I delivered one baby years ago. If everything is normal I shouldn't have a problem. If not—" He didn't want to think about all the things that could go wrong. He'd seen slides, he'd read about placenta previa, fetal distress, prolonged labor....

"Of course not. Only I don't know how helpful I can be. I don't know what to do."

"That makes two of us," he said grimly. He swung by the office, grabbed his computer and chose a CD Rom that gave details of dozens of obstetrical procedures, while Hayley packed all the supplies and instruments he indicated he might need.

"Place is probably filthy," he muttered as they got back into his car. "I didn't know anyone lived out there."

"I didn't, either." Hayley didn't want to admit she'd never been to the dump. It would only reinforce Sam's impression of her as a pampered rich girl who never ventured out of her neighborhood. In fact, her parents would be horrified if they knew she was on her way to the shack near the dump. They said it was a dirty, dangerous area. They would be even more horrified if they knew she was going to deliver a baby with Sam Prentice. They'd be horrified if they knew she was on her way *anywhere* with Sam Prentice.

She was afraid of what they'd find. A wild-eyed old man who didn't want them there, a frightened young woman in pain, who was going to deliver a baby in a dirty shack.

Why was it was so easy for some people? They got pregnant and nine months later they went into labor and delivered a baby. Not that she envied the poor woman and her crazy father. She only felt a twinge of regret for what had happened to herself. Wishing things had been different for her.... But if things had been different she wouldn't be there with Sam on her way to deliver a baby. She wondered who the father was, where he was and how the girl ended up giving birth alone.

"Are you paying attention?" Sam asked, turning on his bright headlights to shine on the dark, empty highway. "Are you watching for the turnoff?"

"Oh, yes...sure. I think it must be up here."

Sam turned abruptly onto an old dirt road, bumping and scraping his high-performance car over potholes. Hayley pressed her hand to her face as a putrid smell filled the air. Finally he came to a screeching halt in front of a tumbledown wooden shack with lights burning behind bare, uncurtained windows.

"Could this be it?" he asked, opening his door and stepping out into the fetid air.

Hayley didn't answer. She didn't know. But she got out, too, and swallowed hard as she surveyed the shack. Instead of helping Sam unload the car, she stood staring at the smoke that poured from the chimney, hearing muted screams from the direction of the shack and wishing she hadn't come. She wouldn't be able to help. She was a wimp. A spoiled rich girl. Oh, she thought she'd changed, but faced with a serious problem, a life-and-death situation, she was a bundle of shaking nerves. Just like that night only a few years ago. When she'd been the one in trouble. She'd been scared, cold, anxious and alone. Tonight she wasn't alone. But nonetheless she was going to be no help at all. She didn't have what it took. The backbone, the courage or the confidence.

"Let's go," Sam said urgently, shoving an instrument case into her hands and nudging her none too gently toward the front door.

"No, I...I can't," she said, dragging her heels. "I'm no good at this."

"How do you know?" he asked, continuing to guide her toward the house. "Have you delivered a baby before?"

She stumbled on a root, bumped into Sam and blinked back the tears that blinded her. "Yes. No. Of course not."

"Then you can do it. I know you. You can do anything you put your mind to." He set his computer and a leather bag on the front porch that had cobwebs hanging from the door frame, put his arm around her and squeezed her shoulders.

She might not have confidence in herself, but he had confidence in her. It made her feel as if she could not only deliver a baby, but perform brain surgery and climb mountains, too, as long as he was there.

She took a deep breath. "Okay, I'm all right now," she whispered.

Sam banged on the door with his fist.

"What the hell?" came a raspy voice above the screams. "What is it now?"

"It's the doctor," Sam yelled. "I'm coming in." He charged through the door, with Hayley behind him, where they found the old man standing in the middle of the living room waving a whisky bottle in his hand.

"Get the hell out of here," he yelled drunkenly. "I don't want you. I want the real doctor, not you."

Seven

"**W**here is she?" Sam demanded, ignoring the man's protests and the whisky bottle he brandished menacingly.

The man jerked a thumb in the direction of the screams and a moment later she and Sam were in a bedroom facing the sight of the teenage girl, writhing on an unmade bed in a tangle of sheets.

Hayley stood staring at the woman, closed her eyes for a second and rocked back and forth on her heels. Though she'd never fainted in her life, she felt as if she would now. She didn't want to see the girl's bloated body, didn't want to hear her ear-splitting screams. She wanted to run out of the house, but Sam was there. Sam was counting on her. Sam was sitting on the edge of the bed, one hand pressing on the girl's abdomen, the other on her forehead.

"Okay, Shawnee, calm down. Everything's going to be okay. I'm a doctor and I'm going to deliver your baby for you," he said.

The girl's screams subsided slightly, and Sam looked over at Hayley. "Don't just stand there, turn on my computer," he said. "And find the kitchen. Boil water. Then get back here."

Her fingers fumbled as she slid his laptop out of its case and flipped the switches.

"Find the CD labeled OB and boot it up."

"What about the water?" she asked.

"Didn't you start the water yet?" he asked irritably. "Then get out the alcohol. I have to sterilize everything."

"I...I—" She didn't know what to do next. Clearly he was accustomed to having his orders obeyed by a highly trained staff, but she didn't know what to do first—find the CD, get out the alcohol or boil water. Sam had turned back to his patient as if Hayley wasn't there. Confident that she'd do what he'd told her. As his professional staff did.

"Take a deep breath," he ordered the woman. "Another...another."

While he was talking to Shawnee in a low, soothing voice, Hayley knew that if she were delivering a baby, if she were in any kind of trouble, she'd want Sam there. Sure he was irritable, but he was also so strong and capable, so sure and so calm. As if he did this every day, even though she knew he'd never done it before, never delivered a baby outside a hospital, with no one to help him except a totally inexperienced person. If only he'd been there the night she'd needed a doctor...someone...anyone. But she'd been alone and terrified. This was no time to dwell on the past, this was the time to show him she was up to the job.

Leaving Sam to take the girl's temperature and her vital signs, Hayley went down the hall to the kitchen, carefully skirting the old man in the living room. She put a pot of water on the stove, then hurried back to find Sam on the floor on his knees, his stethoscope pressed just above the woman's navel.

"You're doing fine," he said to Shawnee with surprising gentleness, then he got up and took Hayley's arm and pulled her into the hall. He grabbed her hands tightly in his and pulled her toward him until his face was so close she could see the worry lines between his eyebrows and into the depths of his dark eyes.

"We've got a little problem," he said under his breath.

Her eyes widened in alarm.

"We've got a breech presentation. He's coming out butt first," he said. "And he's coming fast."

She licked her dry lips. "Is that bad?"

"Could be. If we were in a hospital I'd do a C-section. Not me, but someone would. Someone who's done it a hundred times. But we're not in a hospital. We're going to have to wing it here. First I'm going into the kitchen to scrub, and you're going to find the instructions from the OB CD on breech deliveries, and I'm going to do my damnedest to follow them. Main thing is to keep calm."

"I will," she promised.

"I don't mean you. Of course *you* will. I mean the girl. Keep her calm. Don't let her know she's in trouble. Here's my watch to time her contractions. I'll be right back."

Hayley wanted to scream, Don't leave me alone with her. What if something happens? What if...what if...

Gingerly, very carefully, Hayley perched on the edge of the bed and looked into the girl's face for the first time. She saw pure terror in the eyes staring up at her, heard her gasp for breath. Oh, Lord, what if the baby came out now.

"I'm Hayley, Shawnee," Hayley said, her voice little more than a whisper. "I'm here to help you." The information from the books she'd devoured on birth and babies years ago when she'd thought…she'd hoped…was stored somewhere in the back of her mind. Obviously this poor girl had had no instructions whatsoever. Or any prenatal care, either.

What was it she was supposed to do? Oh, yes. Take deep breaths. Pant. Time the contractions. Suck on ice. Massage the belly. "Don't be afraid," Hayley said. "Doctor Prentice is here to deliver your baby. He's very good. Just relax. Does it hurt very much?"

Shawnee wearily closed her eyes between contractions without answering. What a stupid thing to say. Of course it hurt.

"Take a deep breath," Hayley said, and was encouraged to see the girl do it. Hayley timed the next few contractions with the stopwatch while talking the girl through them. They were coming faster and faster. Where was Sam? When he came back in the room she jumped up from the bed.

"Contractions every two minutes, lasting thirty seconds. Does that help?" she asked.

"Good girl," he said, taking her place at the bedside and doing a quick examination. "Cervix dilated five centimeters. Now tell me what instructions you find under breech deliveries."

Hayley took a seat in the straight-back wooden chair with the computer in her lap and scrolled rapidly through the topics, her fingers icy cold and shaking.

"Well?" he prompted.

"I'm looking, I'm looking," she said. "Here we are. Some physicians feel all breech deliveries should undergo cesarean section because the doctor cannot know if the mother's pelvis will be able to accommodate the bulkiest part of the baby's body.'"

"Fine," he muttered. "Go on, get to the good part."

"Okay, here's something. 'Attempt to shift baby's position by manipulating the uterus manually. A process called an external version. Or do an ultrasound scan to determine if the baby is small enough to pass through the pelvis.'"

"Too late for that. Too late for anything. Here he comes. Get over here right away," he said urgently. "You're going to catch this baby."

"Me? No, I can't. I...I..." But she took a deep breath and knelt on the floor. If Sam thought she could do it, then she could. So when the slippery, squirmy baby came out buttocks first, after what seemed an agonizingly long wait, punctuated by the mother's screams of pain, she was there to catch it while Sam reached into his bag for some clamps. After clamping the umbilical cord in two places, he cut it between the clamps. He took the baby, did a quick exam, then handed it to the mother.

"It's a girl," Hayley said reverently.

"She's okay, isn't she?" she asked shyly.

"She's perfect," he told her with a smile. He looked at Hayley, and their glances locked and held for a long moment. Together they'd brought this baby into the world. They'd participated in a miracle. It wasn't their baby. But in a way it *was* their baby. Because if they hadn't been there...if Sam hadn't come back to New Hope... Her heart swelled and she blinked back the tears that threatened to spill from her eyes. She almost thought Sam's eyes were wet, too. But that couldn't be. He was a doctor. He couldn't cry every time he saved a life or brought a new one into the world.

Hayley cleared her throat and broke eye contact with him. "The instructions say to put an ID bracelet on the baby," she noted.

"I'm fresh out of ID bracelets," he said. "In this case

I don't think there'll be any confusion. We'll let her mother bond with her and then clean everybody up,'' Sam told Hayley, gathering his instruments methodically as if he did it every day.

And he said he didn't know anything about childbirth. Hayley slowly got up off the floor. Her legs were stiff; she was shaking all over. She felt as if she'd just had a baby herself. But she hadn't and wasn't likely to. She gazed down at the mother and the tiny baby sprawled across her chest, and she was filled with longing for what she couldn't have. Her heart contracted as waves of unbecoming envy washed over her.

The rest of the night was a blur in her mind. With the hot water from the stove, and the disinfectant from Sam's black bag, she and Sam cleaned up the baby, the mother and themselves. They found a linen closet and changed the sheets on the mother's bed. When they finally left, the baby was nursing hungrily, and the old man had passed out on the living room couch, snoring loudly, his bottle on the floor beside him.

"I'm sending an ambulance to get the two of them tomorrow," he told Hayley as she got into his car next to him. "The baby needs to be checked out by a pediatrician in Portland."

She nodded and laid her head back against the headrest. She was cold, tired and couldn't shake the mild depression and letdown that followed the excitement of the birth.

"Sorry I yelled at you," he said. "Are you okay?" he asked, turning the heater on and glancing at her as he drove back up the rutted road.

"Just a little postpartum depression," she said lightly as a tear dribbled down her cheek. She turned her face toward the window, but she felt his gaze linger, sensed his surprise, perhaps disappointment at her lack of fortitude.

After all, to him it was just another procedure, another day at the office. But to her... "And a little envy," she added

"You're envious of a teenage, unmarried mother?" he asked incredulously. "She's more likely envious of you. Hayley Bancroft, the cream of New Hope society, with your education and your looks, you've got everything."

"I don't have a baby," she blurted, frantically blinking back the tears that welled up in her eyes as the memories came rushing back. She hadn't cried the night she lost the baby. She shouldn't cry now. But she did. She couldn't stop.

"I didn't know you wanted one," he said with a frown.

"I don't." Her shoulders shook as the tears poured down her face.

"Are you crying?" he asked. He sounded shocked. As if he'd never seen her cry before. As if she was an ice queen. The girl who had everything. Except a baby.

She didn't speak. Couldn't say anything. Her throat was clogged with the effort to stem the tide of pain and envy and tears. He pulled off the highway and stopped the car. He put his hands on her shoulders and turned her toward him. When she kept her eyes on her hands in her lap, he tilted her chin with his hand and brushed a tear from her cheek with the pad of his thumb. His touch was so gentle she cried harder than ever—loud, unladylike, gulping sobs that threatened to swamp them both.

"I'm s-s-sorry," she stammered. All these years. All the tears she'd never shed for herself she was crying now.

"Sorry for what?" he asked.

"For being such a wimp."

"You're not a wimp," he said. Then he gripped her shoulders and kissed away her tears, from her eyes, her cheeks and then he found her mouth. He kissed her gently at first, healing kisses as if she were a wounded dove, so fragile she might break. Then as she got stronger, as she responded like an aroused woman, came hotter, wetter kisses, that stirred her soul and made her heart pound, made her forget the pain and the envy and the sadness. Made her forget everything but him.

He filled her senses with his masculine scent, part doctor, part town bad boy, with the touch of his clever hands, the hands that could save lives and deliver babies and with the pressure of his mouth on hers. He filled her soul with something else, something that felt like love. If she didn't know better, she would have thought…would have hoped…but of course it wasn't love. Sam Prentice didn't love her. He'd forgotten all about her. Never even tried to get in touch with her all these years. It was lust, pure and simple. For the moment it would have to do. It was what she needed. It made her forget about envy, about her longing for a baby.

He pressed her back against the passenger door, and she wound her arms around his neck and returned his kisses, desperate to feel the heat from his body, to inhale the all-male scent of him. To wipe out the memories of the pain of her loss and the loneliness that she'd never forgotten. Never would forget.

These kisses were nothing like those frantic, desperate, clandestine kisses they'd exchanged so long ago. They were adults now, free of constraints, with no one to keep tabs on them. No one who would burst into the playhouse and set off the alarm. No one to set the dogs loose, to chase him over the fence, where he'd ripped his pants before landing safely on the other side, while her parents screamed at him and she'd watched helplessly.

And yet there was something so achingly familiar, so intimate about his kisses, about the way he cupped the back of her head, his fingers threaded through her hair as if they'd never been apart. Even though they'd never really been together. It was as if they belonged together. He kissed her like a hungry man who'd been starving for the past seventeen years. She knew the feeling. She was just as hungry. Even more so. He slid his tongue along the seam of her lips and teased her until a rush of heat filled her body and she opened to him. Welcomed him. Joined him in the most passionate dance of her life. He made her feel reckless and free. As if anything was possible. And it was. At least for tonight.

She wanted to make love to him. She wanted to finish what they'd started so many years ago. Because if she didn't, she would go through the rest of her life as unfulfilled as she had been the past seventeen years. Wanting what she couldn't have. Wanting him. First because he was the town bad boy, and now because he was a high-priced surgeon she couldn't afford. But tonight the playing field was level. They could finally have what they'd been denied so long ago.

She'd spent all this time playing what-if…. What if Grandpa hadn't told the police about him. What if she'd followed him out of town. What if she'd gotten in touch with him years ago. What if he'd come back. He *was* back. Not for ever. Not for long. And certainly not for her. But for now he was back. In her house. In her arms. They wanted each other. Not forever. For now. Tonight.

She knew it; he knew it. So why resist? She didn't. She gave in to the pressure of his mouth and of his big, skillful, surgeon's hands that cradled her face. His kisses were nothing like the kisses of a hot-blooded teenager and yet they were everything like it. Everything that happened in the past was part of what was happening now. She kissed him back with all the passion she'd been saving up for seventeen years.

He moaned in the back of his throat and he dragged her across the seat until she was sitting in his lap.

"Hey," he said, tipping his head back to look at her with heavy-lidded, sexy eyes and slipping his hand under her shirt and her lace bra until he covered her left breast. "I can feel your heart pounding."

She gasped. His hand was cool on her feverish skin. She buried her face in his chest. "Oh, Sam," she murmured against the soft wool of his sweater. "I've missed you." He traced his thumb in concentric circles on her breast, then moved to the other until she couldn't think, couldn't breathe. His hands were so skillful, there was nothing he couldn't do. Nothing he couldn't do to her. She couldn't get enough of him. She wanted more from him. She was frantic now, wanting to get rid of her clothes, all of them. So he could touch her all over the way he was touching her now. But somewhere in the back of her brain she realized the door handle was drilling a hole in the middle of her back. And they were parked off the highway.

"Let's go home," Sam said gruffly, reading her mind. He wanted to devour her with his mouth; he wanted to undress her and make her his, if only for one night. But not here. He took a deep breath and untangled her arms from around his neck and forced himself to place his hands on the steering wheel and drive back to her house. She kept one hand on his thigh, which didn't make anything easier for him. It made him press his foot harder on the gas, it made him reach over and thread his fingers in her hair and pull her as close to him as he could without removing her seat belt. Even though he was flying down the road, pushing his highly tuned engine to go faster, it seemed they'd never get home.

It wasn't until five minutes later that he realized he'd referred to the Bancroft House as home. He hoped Hayley hadn't noticed. Glad her parents hadn't heard him say that. He grimaced as he imagined what they'd say.

"It'll be a cold day in hell before that house is your home, boy," her father would say.

"Take your hands off my daughter," her mother would say. Although at the moment it was Hayley's warm hand on his thigh, sending a shaft of desire coursing through him, so strong he wondered if he'd make it back "home."

He did make it. He parked the car in the driveway. She'd left the lights on in the windows, warm and welcoming.

"Race you to the front door," he said, and let her win.

She leaned against the door, waiting for him, breathless and giddy. He grabbed the key from her hand, unlocked the door and slammed it shut behind them. The house was big and empty, warm and quiet. It smelled like the resin from the pine logs that were piled next to the fireplace. Like lemon furniture polish and cinnamon from the rolls that were rising on the kitchen counter. They stood in the tiled vestibule and studied each other for a long moment. Their haste was forgotten now that they were home. Now that they had the whole night ahead of them.

"You were great tonight, you know that?" he said, his arms crossed casually over his chest. "I'm sorry I yelled at you. I couldn't have done it without you."

"I can't believe you delivered a baby."

"*We* delivered a baby."

She nodded and gave him a small smile. "I was scared."

"Me, too," he admitted. There was another long silence. "Now what?" he asked. Before he grabbed her, swung her over his shoulder and carried her up the stairs two at a time, he had to be sure this was what she wanted. That she was willing to go through with what they'd started a lifetime ago.

"We could have a cup of coffee," she said, looking down at her shoes.

"Or..." he prompted.

"We could take a shower," she said, looking up at him from under her lashes. "I smell like carbolic soap."

"Your place or mine?" he asked.

"Yours," she said, and took his hand to lead him up the stairs.

"Have you thought what your parents would say if they could see you now?" he asked, one arm around her waist. His hand on her hip.

She shook her head. "No."

It was a shower to end all showers. He knew before he even stepped into the large, glassed-in enclosure he would remember this one for a long time. Copious amounts of hot water cascaded over her body as he lathered her with fragrant lavender soap from her neck to her knees, his hand lingering on the valley between her breasts, then sliding down to her warm, slick thighs until her knees buckled and she flung her arms around his shoulders so she wouldn't fall down.

"Sam, please," she muttered as the water beat against her back. "I can't...I can't.... Let me. It's my turn."

He didn't want to, but he let her go, carefully, gingerly, with his hands on her shoulders, so she wouldn't collapse, bracing her until she took the soap from him and started in on him, running her hands across his shoulders, catching the soap in the dark hair on his chest. He didn't know how long he could stand any more of this intense pleasure. He was fully aroused now and he watched while she took her soapy hands and massaged the length of him. With a huge effort, he reached behind and turned the water off.

Outside the shower, in the spacious, steamy bathroom, they toweled each other briskly, but inefficiently, missing large areas of skin, interrupted by the need to exchange heated kisses, until they finally staggered into the bedroom, where the sheepskin rug tickled their bare feet. Hayley crawled under the mosquito netting, and lay back on the soft cotton sheet and smiled up at him. Her skin was pink, her hair damp and her eyes glowing with anticipation. Under that net, she looked like someone out of a harem. He'd never seen anyone as exotic. She'd always been beautiful. But tonight she was intriguing, mysterious. He reminded himself this was Hayley. The Hayley he'd known forever. But he never thought it could happen. Not to him. Not with her. After all these years.

"I've been waiting seventeen years," she said softly. "For you to make love to me, Sam."

His heart hammered. He'd been waiting, too. Waiting seventeen years to hear her say that. He wanted to go slowly. So she'd savor, enjoy. He wanted her to feel it had been worth the wait. He already knew it would be.

If he'd thought she would be shy and wait for him to make the first move, he was mistaken. With a gleam in her eye she tossed the netting aside and reached to dim the lamp on the nightstand. When he braced his arms on the quilt to loom over her, she rubbed her fingers softly through the dark whorls of chest hair, exploring with her fingertips the hair, the skin, the muscles until he was ready to explode.

When her hands strayed lower to the juncture of his thigh and his belly, he knew he had only seconds before his control snapped. "I hope you know what you're doing," he said.

She smiled, and he knew that she knew exactly what she was doing.

He groaned and covered her mouth with his. His tongue imitated the thrusts of his body as she guided him inside her with her soft hand, until she sheathed him as if she was made for him. She was slick and hot and ready. Just as hot and ready as he was. His thrusts came faster and faster, so strong he was afraid he'd hurt her. But she wanted more. She told him so. So much for taking it slow and easy. So much for foreplay.

Hayley lost control. Her hips were moving in time with his, matching him thrust for thrust. She had hoped to spend time exploring Sam's body, fulfilling all the fantasies she'd had for half of her life. But now that he was here, now that he was inside her, filling her, pushing her toward the edge, faster and faster, she flung her arms out and made sounds of joy, of pleasure, of excitement. She couldn't stop, didn't want to stop. She wanted it to go on forever. The intensity was building, building until her body tensed, and she clenched around him with a cry of ecstasy.

He shouted as he climaxed, his voice filled the room and echoed through the house. Then he collapsed on top of her, his weight and his welcome warmth pressing her down, covering her body. His face was wedged between her neck and shoulder. She wrapped her arms around his neck and held him tight. As if she could keep him there, hold him there forever.

He rolled over on his side, keeping her close with one arm, rising to draw the comforter up over them with his free hand. He was so close she could hear his heart beat in time with hers, feel his skin damp with perspiration and see the lines around his mouth relax as he closed his eyes. They were joined hip to hip. Face-to-face, they shared a pillow. She tucked her knee between his legs. He groaned—with pleasure she hoped. But she wasn't sure.

"Sam?"

"Uh-huh."

"How do you feel?"

"Tired," he muttered, and then he fell asleep.

If she was hoping for a declaration of undying love, or even a comment on what to her was an earthshaking event, she knew better. Sam would never be the demonstrative type. He didn't know how. Despite his demanding profession he'd obviously had time for women, the kind who didn't make demands. Who didn't want a home and children. The way she did. She sighed and matched his even breathing to her own, wishing she could match his insouciance, his casual attitude about relationships and his skepticism about love, because it would make things so much easier.

In the morning she slipped out of bed early to go clamming. Though he said he would go, she didn't want to ask him. Besides, he'd promised to order the ambulance for the new mother and baby. After gathering the clothes she'd left in a pile in his bathroom, she paused naked at the bedroom door and took a last look at his sleeping body sprawled under the comforter. The sheets were probably still warm where she'd finally slept. The pillow still indented where her head was.

With her clothes in her arm, she had to grip the doorknob with her free hand to keep from crawling back into that bed, to absorb the warmth from his body, to wake him with a kiss, to make love with him again, this time slowly and luxuriously. The way she'd meant to do last night. She stood there for a long moment, willing him to sense her presence at the door, to realize she'd left, to feel the loss of her body, wake up, to throw back the sheet and tell her to get back in bed. But he didn't. He continued to sleep, damn his insensitive hide. So she went to her room, dressed in old jeans and a sweatshirt, found her bucket and shovel and drove to the beach.

The sun was just rising in a partly cloudy sky, sending

shafts of pale sunlight onto the wide beach. The tide was low as promised, and her friends were there ahead of her. The flat, wet sand stretched for miles, and the smell of brine filled her senses and helped cleared her mind of Sam and the magic they'd shared the night before. Or had they shared anything but a physical coupling? Had it been only one-sided? Had it meant anything to Sam but getting it on with his high school girlfriend who hadn't really been his girlfriend? Would he ever say anything, or just pretend it had never happened? Or would he—

"Hayley," Donna called, with one foot on her shovel while her husband wandered farther down the beach. "Snap out of it. There are clams everywhere, just begging you to dig them up and put them into your bucket, and you're somewhere else in a dream world. This couldn't have anything to do with the return of Sam Prentice, could it?"

"Of course not," she said indignantly.

"Didn't you have a crush on Sam in high school?" Donna asked.

"I might have," Hayley admitted, "along with every other girl in our class. He was forbidden fruit."

"That's for sure. I was scared to death of him," Donna said. "Besides being the best-looking guy in town, he had to be the most dangerous. The kind every mother warns her daughter about. Is it true he stole a car, was arrested and got knifed the night before graduation?"

Hayley concentrated on a bubble just under the sand, indicating the presence of a clam below the surface, and dug her shovel in. "That was a long time ago," she said, neither affirming nor denying it. "He's changed."

"Except for one thing," Donna said tossing a clam into her bucket with a loud clank. "He's still gorgeous and he still looks dangerous."

If she only knew how dangerous he was. Dangerous to Hayley's well-being, dangerous to her mental health. No, she couldn't disagree with that assessment. She decided to devote herself to digging clams instead of discussing Sam.

"How did you ever talk him into coming back here?" Donna asked after they'd combed the beach, filling their buckets for a while in companionable silence. "I heard he's a big-time surgeon in San Francisco." No need to ask who "he" was. Donna was fixated on Sam. Hayley couldn't blame her. Sam had that effect on people, especially women.

"Just luck," she said lightly. "We needed a doctor. I looked everywhere first, then I remembered that Sam was an M.D. And I happened to contact him just as he needed to take some time off from his job. Something not so stressful as surgery. A different atmosphere. Of course, he won't stay here forever."

"Of course not," Donna said with a quick glance at Hayley. As if she thought she'd catch Hayley with a tear in her eye or a catch in her voice at the thought of Sam leaving New Hope to go back to his real life. Instead Hayley flashed her a quick but not quite sincere smile.

"Six months max," Hayley said, as much to remind herself as to tell Donna.

"Where is he, by the way?" her friend asked.

"He had a house call to make or he would be here."

"I was afraid to mention it. I thought maybe he'd find our simple pleasures a little too simple," Donna said.

"Oh, no. Not at all," she lied. She didn't want anyone else in town to know how Sam felt about New Hope. She wanted them to accept him and for Sam to feel welcome and needed. That way he'd have time to change his mind and stay forever. Sure he would. "He just hasn't had time yet for anything but getting the office in shape. Last night after we saw you he delivered a baby.'' She yawned as a blanket of fatigue settled over her. Her eyelids were heavy, her body felt like she'd been run through a roller. "I'm tired. I've got enough clams. I think I'll go home.''

"Why don't you bring your clams and come over tonight for a clambake. And bring Sam, if he's free," Donna suggested. "If he doesn't have another baby to deliver.''

"I'll see," she said cautiously. She hated to guarantee that Sam would appear anywhere.

When she got home, Sam was in the kitchen pouring himself a cup of coffee that he'd brewed himself. Looking and acting as if he belonged there. She set her bucket on the floor and for one magic moment she imagined what it would be like if he did live there. If he was there for her. In her kitchen and in her heart. If he could walk to work. If she could help him out at the office and he could help her out at the house. The lines in his forehead would disappear. He'd laugh with her, make love with her and they'd raise a family in this house as she was meant to do.

Her heart skipped a beat. She forced herself to blank out such treacherous thoughts. They would only lead to heartbreak. She'd already made one disastrous marriage. She wasn't about to try again. Not with Sam, not with anybody. As if he'd want to. He could hardly wait to get out of New Hope and back to where he belonged.

She made herself forget she'd ever made love to him or slept with him all night. She told herself to think of him as a guest. Or as a doctor. Anything but what he was— the man she'd been in love with ever since she could remember.

He was wearing jeans, his hair was standing on end, and his eyes were bleary. He was still the best-looking man she'd ever seen. She wanted to throw herself in his arms, run her hands through his hair and kiss him. But she didn't; she just stood there looking at him.

"Coffee?" he asked, getting up to take a cup from her cupboard as if he was the host and she was the guest.

Eight

She nodded and opened the door to the patio and wandered outside. After several weeks of rain and clouds, she wanted to see some sun, feel it soak into her bones. After crying more tears than she ever had in one night, she was ready to dry out. Sam filled her cup, added cream and sugar and followed her outside where he set both cups on the glass-topped table on the brick terrace.

"Thank you, I need that," she said, feeling secretly pleased and encouraged by such a simple thing—he'd remembered how she liked her coffee. She couldn't help it. She'd given herself to him heart and soul last night and she was desperate for a sign that it was as special for him as for her. So far she couldn't tell.

"Get an early start?" he asked, sitting across the table from her and stirring his coffee.

"Very early. You were still asleep."

He nodded. If she didn't know better she would have

thought the tight lines at the corner of his mouth indicated his annoyance, that he minded her leaving so early, before he woke up. But that couldn't be. That was wishful thinking. This was Sam Prentice, consummate loner. Surely he was accustomed to waking up alone. Just as she was. The difference was, she didn't want to.

"Did you make your house call? How was the baby?" she asked.

"Baby's doing fine. Actively nursing. Content. Mother seemed a little anemic, I gave her some iron supplements. I also called the ambulance and sent them both to Portland to be checked out.

"I had a talk with the old man. He was about to kick them out. I didn't like his attitude, frankly."

"Toward you?" she said.

"Toward me, toward his daughter and toward his granddaughter," he said.

"Where will they go?"

"To Ms. Maudie's boarding house. Still in operation, as you said. And luckily she has room."

"But...but...how will Shawnee afford to stay there, and what will become of her and her baby?"

"Her rates are very reasonable," he said. Hayley knew who was going to pay. It was Sam. Sam who was also going to pay for the ambulance. Sam, who'd hated to swallow his pride and accept charity himself for years, was now in a position to give it. She hoped Shawnee was more gracious than Sam had been when he'd been on the receiving end. She remembered how he'd flatly turned down offers of clothing and even free lunches at school, saying he didn't need anything or anybody. He preferred to wear old threadbare shirts and go hungry to accepting charity.

"What will become of them, I don't know," he continued. "Shawnee will need some help to get on her feet.

Maybe from the baby's father. For the present they'll be clean and fed and comfortable. And the old man is out of the picture. He wants nothing to do with them. And I was able to settle an old score." Sam shifted in his chair. "It seems my father cheated him out of some money during a card game some years ago."

"He could be lying," Hayley suggested.

"He could be, but I paid him off, anyway. And then some. Enough for a ticket out of town, if that's what he wants. Or if he stays he's not to harass his daughter."

"Or his granddaughter," she added, wishing she'd been there to see the baby. "How did the baby look today?"

"Good. She'll bring her in to the office next week when they get back so you can see her." He gave Hayley a half smile and stretched his legs out in front of him. Hayley tilted her head back against the wrought-iron chair back and looked at the puffy clouds that floated in the blue sky above.

"Guess what she named the baby," he said.

"Don't tell me she named her Sam."

"Nope. Hayley."

"She named her after me? I don't believe it." Her eyes widened, and she felt a rush of pride and envy. The surge of emotion caught her by surprise. The girl had named her baby after her. That was sweet, but no reason to get all teary-eyed. There were other reasons to get teary-eyed. One good reason was that Sam seemed to have forgotten what had happened between them last night.

"She appreciated what you did for her," Sam said.

"You delivered her baby. I didn't do anything," she insisted.

"You did a lot. I couldn't have done it without you. You had all the right instincts. That'll come in handy someday. When you have your own baby." He said it so casually. As if it was a foregone conclusion that she would have a baby someday. When it was her conclusion that she wouldn't.

"You wouldn't say that if you knew..." she said, and then wished she'd kept her mouth shut.

"But I *don't* know."

There was a long silence while she debated whether she should tell him at all or how much she should tell him if she did. She didn't want to tell him anything. On the other hand she felt an overwhelming compulsion to tell him everything. Like a rolling stone that was gathering momentum. Every time he spoke, every time he looked at her with his dark, all-knowing, all-seeing eyes she wanted to open her mouth and let it all out.

"It's a long story," she said hesitantly.

"I'm not going anywhere," he said, crossing his arms behind his head.

She took a deep breath. "I wanted to have children. I always wanted to have children."

"I remember," he said. "You vowed you were going to live right here in this house one day with your own family. That's what you said."

She nodded. "And I remember you made fun of my lack of serious goals in life. You didn't think I was ambitious enough. You said I was a throwback to another era. A June Cleaver. You thought since I was good at math, I ought to be an astronaut."

He laughed. The first time she'd heard him laugh since...forever. Lines etched themselves at the corners of his eyes. She had to force herself to stay in her chair. She wanted to jump up and throw her arms around him. To congratulate him for showing he was human. But he wouldn't like that.

"Did I say that?" he asked. "I was full of myself, wasn't I?"

"You knew you weren't going to stay here. You said you were going to get the hell out of town and become a doctor or a lawyer and be respectable and make a lot of money. And you did it."

"Well, at least you came back, and you've got the house you wanted," he said.

She nodded. "Yes, but..."

"No baby," he said.

"No baby and no husband," she said, keeping her voice as level as she could when inside, her stomach was churning. She hated admitting she'd made such a terrible error in judgment in choosing a husband. She wanted Sam to admire her, not feel sorry for her, but after she told this story, he would have only pity for her. Now that she'd gone this far, as much as she didn't want to, she had to tell the whole story. The story she'd kept to herself all these years. It was like a dormant volcano whose time had come to erupt.

"Despite my modest ambitions, Sam, it seems like I'm not destined to have it all, after all," she said gazing off wistfully across the lawn to the badminton court. "The man I married wasn't interested in living in the 'boondocks,' as he called New Hope. Although he was an environmentalist, he really was a city person. And of course he couldn't really do his environmental work here. So we lived in Portland where he could be most effective in the organization. I understood that. I was involved in it, too. It was certainly worth my giving up my dream of coming back here to save the...the...whatever the cause was we were working on at the time." She leaned forward in her chair and gazed earnestly into Sam's eyes. "I believed in him. And the work we were all doing. It wasn't a sacrifice.''

"So what was the problem?'' Sam asked, regarding her with all the sympathy he would have for a patient whose history he was taking in order to make a diagnosis. She already knew what the diagnosis would be. A major case of immaturity complicated by a lack of direction.

She took a deep breath. There was no need to go any further. She'd unburdened her soul enough. And Sam was only being polite, leaning forward slightly in his chair, fixing his gaze on her face, the way he'd do with any patient.

But she wasn't his patient. She was the woman he'd made love to the night before. Instead of shrugging it off, she blurted, "There was no problem—until I got pregnant. At least I didn't think there was a problem.'' Now that she'd started, she couldn't stop. Couldn't stop until the whole story came out. "I realized later how wrong I'd been. I'd assumed he wanted a baby. He didn't. He'd assumed I was on the pill. I wasn't. He said children would interfere with our work. He thought I knew that. We wouldn't be able to take chances, chain ourselves to trees and so forth. He was right.

"He said it was stupid of me to have assumed... He was right again. It *was* stupid. It seemed we never had time to talk about anything personal. It was always the cause of the moment—the old-growth redwood trees, the smoggy air, the polluted water, the endangered field mice. Never us. But that's no excuse for my making such a colossal mistake, such a total error in judgment.''

"What happened?'' he asked.

She paused and gazed off across the lawn toward the badminton court. "I lost the baby.'' She struggled to keep the tears at bay. To keep secure the high, impenetrable wall around her emotions that she'd constructed there three years ago. And succeeded, just barely.

"Why, what happened?"

"I don't know why. Why does anyone miscarry in the first trimester? Just one of those things. They said it could have been stress or it just wasn't meant to be. And then I got a divorce."

She didn't look at Sam but she felt his eyes on her, felt the sympathy emanating from him, just as surely as she felt the warmth of the sun on her bare arms. She wanted to let it soak in, to let it warm her skin as well as her heart. But she was afraid. Afraid he wouldn't understand.

She prayed he wouldn't ask for any details. She hoped he'd leave her a little self-respect. She didn't want to talk about the night it happened. The night she lost the baby.

"I mean what happened that night?"

"That night?" He *would* have to ask. Might as well get it over with, once and for all. So she plunged in. "I was home alone, having terrible back pains, bleeding like crazy. I called Todd but he was at a city council meeting waiting his turn to speak on saving the whales and couldn't leave. I finally called 911. An ambulance came and took me to the hospital. I...I lost the baby, that's all. No one knows why. They patched me up, did a D and C and released me the next day. That was the end of that. And that was the end of my marriage." She was proud of the way she'd told the story, so calmly and so dispassionately. She was surprised how telling it to Sam was easier than she'd imagined. She felt a profound sense of relief. After bottling it up all this time, it was finally over.

"You still want a baby, don't you?" he asked, his gaze never leaving her face.

"It's a little late. I'm thirty-five."

"I know how old you are," he said brusquely. "Women are having babies in their forties, you know."

"It helps to be married."

"It's not too late for that, either," he said.

"I'll keep that in mind," she said, and stood to pick up their empty coffee cups. Her head was pounding. She was exhausted from this conversation. Which was too one-sided to be called a conversation. A confession was more like it. Sam had an answer for everything. He always did. But there was no answer for the fact that she was no closer to achieving her dream of raising her own children here in this house in New Hope than she had been at high school graduation. No closer to having kids who'd run around the garden, play in the playhouse or swing from the rubber tire.

She had to get away from Sam. If she stayed another minute in his company she would blurt out something about last night. She would ask him if it meant anything to him. Something totally inappropriate. But he followed her into the kitchen.

"Get any clams?" he asked.

"A lot. A whole bucket. And so did Donna. By the way, they invited me and you and the clams over for dinner tonight."

"Are you sure they want me?"

"Of course." She paused at the kitchen door. "The most famous delinquent that ever lived in New Hope returns a successful surgeon, who out of the goodness of his heart agrees to treat the local denizens until they find another country doc. They think you're fascinating."

"Fascinating," he repeated with a sardonic smile as he walked to the kitchen door and trapped her in the room by bracing his hands against the door frame. "Do *you* think I'm fascinating, too?" he asked, his eyes narrowed, his mouth only a few dangerous inches from hers. Oh, Lord, this was not what she wanted. She wanted answers not action. She wanted to know how he felt about her, if he thought he could get away with making love to her at night and act as though nothing happened the next day. He was so close she felt his breath on her cheek. So close she could smell his hair and his skin. So close she wanted...she wanted...she wanted him to kiss her again. To get lost in the ecstasy of his kiss, feel his arms around her, his body pressed against hers, his heart beating in time to hers.

"Yes, I think you're fascinating," she admitted reluctantly, her eyes looking anywhere but into his. "Is that all you want to know?" she asked.

"No. I want to know why you left me this morning. No good-morning, no goodbye. Not even a goodbye kiss. You used to have better manners."

"I didn't want to wake you. You'd had a hard night," she said as a flush crept up her neck and flooded her face.

"Is that what you call it?" he asked, a wry smile tugging at his lips. "I call it an incredible night." He brushed his lips across hers, teasing her, testing her. She was badly afraid she'd fail any test he gave her. But she had to pass this test or drop it now.

"What do you want from me, Sam?" she asked, ducking her head and looking up at him from under her lashes.

Sam took a long moment to consider. He knew what he wanted. He wanted her. He'd wanted her since the first day he'd seen her. He wanted her yesterday, today and tomorrow. But especially he wanted her now. He wanted to make love to her on the kitchen counter and on the warm bricks of the patio in the sun. He wanted to carry her up the stairs and back to his bed. He tilted her chin with his thumb and kissed her again, increasing the pressure until he felt her lips soften and her resistance begin to melt.

But instead of throwing her arms around his neck, she turned her head and broke the kiss. "That's what I thought," she said. "You want me. For old-time's sake. For a diversion. For a few months."

"I didn't say that," he said, lines furrowing his brow.

"You didn't have to."

"What do you want from *me,* Hayley? Love, marriage, kids? It's not going to happen." He didn't know why he had to spell it out. She knew him. She knew the kind of life he led.

She pressed her lips together tightly before she spoke, as if she was holding back a torrent of angry words. "I know that," she said finally between stiff lips. "So before we go any further, let's just agree that we had one good night together. Which we'd had coming for many years. Which we needed, to show ourselves that the chemistry was still there. Let's admit that the reason it was so…so good, was our history. The baggage we've been carrying around all these years. That now we've got it out of our systems, we can go back to being doctor and assistant, old friends, whatever…but not lovers. Because if we continue—"

"If we continue, what will happen?" he asked. "I, for one, haven't gotten it out of my system. Good night? You call it a 'good night'? I call it an incredible night. I still want you. I want another incredible night with you. Many more nights. I admit I never forgot you. I thought about you, wondered about you and compared every other woman with you."

"So that's it," she said, her eyes steely. "You only want to continue this…this affair to get me out of your system so you can quit comparing the women in your life

with me. You want to be able to forget me once and for
all by prolonging this affair until you're bored or you leave
here, whichever comes first. Until you've had enough of
me just like all the other women who pass through your
life. Then you'll go back to San Francisco and pick up
where you left off.''

"What's wrong with that?" he asked.

"Nothing," she said, putting both hands against his
chest and pushing him away from her. "Nothing at all.
Except that I've made one big mistake with a man I badly
misjudged. I like to think I'm smarter now. At least I'm
older. And I'm not going along with your plan. I'm bailing
out right now. I don't need an affair with you to get you
out of my system. You're already long gone. Whatever we
had is over. It was nothing, anyway. A teenage crush. An
infatuation between two people who were forbidden to
each other. That's all.''

"You've got it all figured out, don't you?" he said,
glaring at her. She'd just summed up feelings that didn't
apply to him at all, and it made him damned mad. "Let
me tell you whatever I felt for you was *not* a teenage crush.
And whatever we felt for each other is *not* over. Not by a
long shot." He grabbed her by the shoulders and kissed
her so hard he was afraid he'd hurt her. But after a quick
gasp of surprise, she dug her fingers into his shoulders and
kissed him back—just as fiercely as he'd kissed her. There
was no love there, no affection, just plain retaliation.

When she finally broke the kiss and wrenched herself
away from him, he watched her leave the kitchen, feeling
as if he'd just lost the battle. But one battle didn't make a
war. He wasn't about to surrender. She couldn't pretend
she didn't feel anything for him. Not after last night.
Maybe it was just lust. If it was, so be it. It was good
enough for him.

Sam pressed his forehead against the wall and stood in the kitchen listening to Hayley's footsteps on the stairs, heard her slam her bedroom door just as firmly as she'd shut him off a few minutes before. He knew he was too restless to stay in the house, too frustrated to sit still, too wound up to lie in the sun on Hayley's patio and wonder what she was doing and when she would come down.

He walked out the front door not knowing where he was going or why. He just knew he had to get away from the Bancroft House, the symbol of everything he'd ever wanted and couldn't have. At this stage of his life he could have almost any woman he wanted. He could afford to buy almost any house he wanted. Then why did he continue to want her, to be bogged down in a love-hate relationship with this house and this town? Because she was a symbol and so was her house and so was New Hope. They symbolized small-town manners and morals and standards. Standards and manners he could never live up to. Until now. The question was did he want to? Did he want to belong to a place that had kicked him out long ago. The answer was no, of course he didn't.

Where did he belong? He didn't really belong to San Francisco. Oh, he was happy there. He had his work there. He'd found satisfaction there. But he'd never felt as if he belonged. Not the way Hayley knew she belonged to New Hope.

Without knowing where he was going or why, he walked toward the ocean beach where the waves crashed against the shore. As a kid he'd always found what solace he could at the beach. Away from the turmoil of his house. His mother and her men. The occasional appearance of his drunken father. The roar of the sea was soothing after the clamor of angry voices. He'd pick up an odd shell or a water-polished stone, or sometimes a piece of driftwood.

He once gave Hayley a shell because it made him think of her, pink and polished and perfect. She wouldn't remember it, but he did. He remembered the way her eyes lit up, the way she ran her finger over the surface as if it was something special.

He took off his shoes and walked for miles along hard-packed wet sand, trying to shake the image of Hayley in his bed last night, the sound of her cries of pleasure, the touch of her skin. She thought he was selfish, that he was using her, but that wasn't true. Yes, he wanted to be able to leave New Hope this time without regrets, without unfinished business, but hadn't she wanted to begin an affair just as much as he did?

The answer had to be yes. The difference was she wanted to break it off now. After one night with him, she'd had enough. She thought now they could live under the same roof for six months and pretend they were just old friends. Act as if there was no electricity in the air when they were together, as though he was a guest at her B&B and nothing more. Eat her muffins in the morning, work alongside of her, sleep down the hall from her and not go crazy from wanting her. And he did want her. More than he had as a crazy teenager, more than yesterday when he didn't know, only suspected, what a warm, generous, giving lover she was. For him there was no going back. He had to convince her to move forward with him. To explore this thing they had together, always had had and, God help them, always would have.

The sun beat down on his shoulders; the salt spray dampened his shirt. After walking for miles, he finally stopped to watch a man and a boy surf fishing. The two were bent over a bucket of bait. The man was showing his son how to put a chunk of sardine on the hook. Pants rolled up to the knees, eleven-foot poles over their shoulders, they walked to the edge of the surf as the tide receded.

Sam sat on the sand, wrapped his arms around his legs and watched the man put his arms around his son and guide the child's arm back to cast out as far as he could. Then they reeled their line in and started over. Over and over they repeated this action until the line was out. The man helped the boy stick his pole into the sand and repeated the process with his own pole. Then they sat next to each other on the sand, shoulders touching, to watch and wait for a strike.

Sam felt his throat tighten. The affection between father and son, the companionship of the two, was obvious from across the sand and filled him with a sense of loss that hurt like a shaft through the heart. As a kid he'd often surf fished, coming out to the beach at low tide, but not with a surf rod and reel. He'd had to make do with a stick and a string and a can of worms he'd dug up. Of course he'd had no father to show him how to fish. And no mother around to fry the fish when he came home. He didn't care. He still loved fishing.

He didn't need a father. He'd figured out surf fishing for himself by watching others. Such a simple thing. A man and a boy fishing together. If he had a son he would teach him to fish. They would spend Saturday mornings on the beach, the wind ruffling the boy's hair, the waves smacking against their legs. He'd told Hayley he didn't know how to be a father, since he'd never had one. But today it seemed easy. Easy and so obtainable he could almost reach out and grab it for himself. Fatherhood. The unconditional love of a father for a child. He'd never had a father, but he could have a child. If...if...

As he watched, the boy's pole bent gracefully down, and the kid got to his feet and jumped up and down with excitement. Sam stood and smiled, held his breath and hoped it would be a big, beautiful striped bass. Big enough to take home. Big enough to fry for dinner.

Then he couldn't watch anymore. He turned and walked back the way he'd come. He'd seen enough. He'd seen himself on that beach. Himself as a boy, himself as a man. To be the man he wanted to be, he had to grow up. He had to make peace with Hayley. The girl who'd once said she loved him. The girl he'd never forgotten. If he didn't do that, the past seventeen years had been a waste. She was right. He'd intended to use her, to make love to her until he didn't need her anymore. She deserved better than that. And deep down he already knew that exorcising her out of his mind and his memory was an unattainable goal.

Hayley spent the afternoon in a frenzy of activity, vacuuming, dusting and polishing. It was her antidote for the depression that nagged at her following their argument. The argument that left her shaken and filled with doubts. She wondered if she was right. Would it really make any difference if she had a six-month affair with Sam or a one-night affair? Yes, she was going to have a hard time getting over him no matter what. How could it be any worse?

From her bedroom window she'd watched Sam walk down the driveway and cross the street, his hands jammed into his pockets, his collar turned up. The image she remembered from out of the past. He looked as angry and upset as she was. He couldn't understand her reasoning. She thought about running after him, trying once again to explain her position. But he was so stubborn, he wouldn't listen.

She hoped he wouldn't come back in time for dinner with her friends. She had nothing more to say to him. And she didn't want to pretend all evening that everything was fine between them. He'd made it clear he wanted a six-month affair with her, then he would walk out of her life forever and leave her behind. It wasn't going to be easy, watching him leave for the second time in her life, but if she cut off the affair now, she'd be in better shape to get along without him. At least that was the theory. She replayed their argument over and over in her mind to the whir of the vacuum. She wasn't ready to take it up again in person, so she got ready early to go across town for dinner.

But she wasn't in luck. Just as she was about to walk out the front door, in her favorite black stretch pants and a white sweater, the bucket of clams in her hand, he appeared in the driveway, sunburned, windblown...so ruggedly handsome, so different from the Sam she'd encountered in his office, he took her breath away. Damn him.

"Time to go?" he asked, and before she could answer he said, "Be right with you, after a quick shower."

She stood in the doorway without speaking. Wanting to say, you're too late. I can't wait. I'm going without you. But she didn't say anything as he brushed by her. She sat on the front steps and waited for him. Just as he knew she would.

When he came out the front door ten minutes later, he looked even better, in khaki pants and a black T-shirt. He smelled like the sandalwood soap she'd put in his bathroom, and his hair was slicked back behind his ears, leaving his suntanned face, his firm jaw, his dark eyes to stand out in stark relief. He picked up the bucket of clams and put them in the trunk of his car. She strapped herself into the bucket seat of his expensive sports car and gave directions to her friends' house.

"Have a nice day?" he asked as they drove down Main Street. As if nothing had happened. As if she was Grandma

Pringle rocking back and forth on her front porch on Fourth Street as he strolled by.

"Lovely," she said, staring straight ahead at the stores along the street. She could be just as unconcerned, just as casual as he could. "You?"

"I went for a walk on the beach."

"Nice day for it," she said.

"You should have come with me," he said.

"I had work to do," she said. As if he'd invited her along.

"You work too hard," he said.

"That's funny, coming from you," she noted. "The original workaholic."

"What's the point of living on the coast if you don't go to the beach on a day like this?" he asked.

"I went clamming this morning," she reminded him.

"Next time I'll come with you," he said. "I don't think I'll have any more babies to check out."

"Sam…"

"I'm sorry about what I said this morning," he said. "You were right and I was wrong. I was totally out of line suggesting we have an affair while I'm here. We've got it out of our systems now, and we can be friends." He reached over and stuck out his hand. She shook it quickly. What else could she do but let him take her hand in his for a brief moment and pretend she felt nothing? No electric current flowing from his hand to hers, no accelerated heartbeat just from the friction of his skin against hers.

She folded her arms across her waist and turned to look out the side window, trying to still the frantic beating of her heart. From just one apology and a handshake. She was pathetic really. All he had to do was apologize and shake her hand and she was a basket case. Her forehead puckered as she tried to reconcile this side of Sam to the

Sam she already knew. This was a relaxed, easygoing Sam, who could admit he was wrong. She didn't know what to say so she didn't say anything. But her thoughts were spinning around in her head as she tried to figure him out.

At the Lambs' house, an old Victorian on Beech Street that they were remodeling, Sam surprised her further by being out-and-out charming. She asked herself what had happened to the chip on his shoulder. Oh, he'd been polite to them in the restaurant last night, but nothing like this. He asked questions, he answered questions, but kept the conversation rolling by drawing them out, getting them talking about their lives and why they'd come back to New Hope.

"I didn't know what to do when I got out of college," Pete said. "What do you do with a major in sociology? I never thought I'd come back here, but after I looked around I decided there wasn't a nicer place to live than New Hope. There's something to be said about coming home. Then my dad retired and left me the hardware store, so it was an easy choice. Fortunately, Donna agreed with me."

Hayley held her breath, knowing Sam was thinking that his dad left him nothing, not even one happy memory. But if Sam thought that, he didn't show it. Instead he recalled that when he was a kid Mr. Lamb had donated his time and materials to install a new playground at the elementary school, which illustrated what a hardworking, generous man Jonah Lamb had been. Pete looked surprised and pleased that Sam had remembered.

"And of course it's a good place to bring up kids," Donna said in answer to Sam's question.

Hayley looked up from the wine cooler they'd poured her. Donna and Pete had been trying to have kids since they got married years ago. But if she'd finally gotten pregnant, she hadn't told Hayley about it.

"We haven't told anyone yet, not until we're sure, but we filed for adoption, and we think, we hope, we're getting a baby."

Hayley set her drink down, and her eyes filled with tears. Tears of happiness for her friend. Tears of envy for herself. Donna was thirty-five and she was going to get a baby of her own. Sam shot her a look that said, see, thirty-five *isn't* too late. But Donna was happily married to her hometown, high school sweetheart. Another day, another baby. For someone else. She choked back her unbecoming jealousies. "Oh, Donna, that's wonderful. I'm so happy for you. When will you...who will you..."

"It's a teenage, unmarried girl in Portland. Your grandfather was working on getting us a baby through his contacts. When he died I didn't know what to do, where to turn, but suddenly our number came up." Hayley could see Donna was radiantly happy as she reached for her husband's hand. It was plain to see how much in love they still were by the way they looked in each other's eyes.

The clams, which Donna had steamed in white wine and parsley and garlic, were delicious. Sam said next time he'd bring a striped bass. Just as soon as he bought himself some fishing gear. Pete said he had some for sale at the store and he'd go fishing with Sam himself. Hayley didn't believe what she was hearing. Sam and Pete going fishing together? Sam, the loner, seemed glad to have the company. Or was he just being polite?

On the way home he said, "Nice people."

"Yes, they are."

When they got back to the house, Hayley braced herself for something—what, she didn't know. Another argument? Another seduction? Sam was being someone else. She didn't know what to expect from him next. What she least expected was that he'd go right to his room after he thanked her for including him in the dinner with her friends. No sarcasm, no criticism of New Hope, stated or implied. And no smoldering looks, no flirtation, no kisses. She was relieved...or was that disappointment she felt?

"Are you feeling all right, Sam?" she asked from the bottom of the stairway.

"Fine," he said from the landing. "Why?"

"You didn't really know Pete or Donna in high school, did you?" she asked, her eyebrows drawn together.

"No, and I didn't want to. She was your friend. He was a big athlete. I was jealous of them both. I assumed they were rich snobs."

"Rich? His father owned the hardware store."

"To me that was rich." He took another step up the stairs, obviously tired of this discussion, obviously trying to escape from her.

She nodded. It was insensitive of her not to realize the contrast Sam had felt between the other kids and himself. Also insensitive not to realize he was trying to get away from her. He didn't want to spend any more time talking to her.

"How would eggs Benedict be in the morning?" she asked.

"Sounds good, but you don't have to do that. All I need is coffee."

"This is a bed and breakfast. I can't let you go to work without breakfast. You're my guest," she reminded him as he disappeared from view down the hall. She stood there, her arm on the polished oak railing, listening, thinking, wondering. But the longer she stood there, as the quiet of her house closed around her, the more bewildered she was at the change in her guest.

She made eggs Benedict the next morning. The morning after that she made French toast, and so it went for the next few weeks. He ate the breakfasts she cooked while reading the newspaper. Not the *San Francisco Chronicle* that he was used to, but the local gazette filled with local news about the tourist industry, logging and fishing. Each morning he thanked her and walked to the office. They worked together in the afternoons, seeing an increasing number of patients each day. In between appointments, Sam would be at his computer, writing or reading.

Fortunately she had a good number of real, paying guests to keep her busy. If she hadn't, she might have been even more lonely than she was. Missing Sam's teasing, his questions, his recollections of the past they shared. Around the office he was scrupulously careful to avoid being thrown together with her. Even Mattie noticed.

Hayley didn't see him in the evenings. She assumed he ate at the diner, but she didn't ask and he didn't tell. She would have liked to cook dinner for him, but she was afraid to suggest it. Afraid it would send the wrong signal. That she was lonely. That she wanted his company. That she missed him. That she'd made a mistake when she told him one night with him was enough.

Nine

"**Y**ou and Sam getting along okay?" Mattie asked in a half whisper, giving a furtive look over her shoulder one day as Hayley came in to replace her at noon.

"Of course, why?"

"Thought you'd at least be going to lunch together, or consorting together after work."

"Mattie," Hayley said with a patient smile. "I knew you wouldn't approve of anything like that."

"When did my opinion ever stop you from doing something?"

Hayley let that go. "Besides, he's got patients to see. I've got a business to run. I told you there's nothing going on between us."

"Why not?" the nurse asked, taking her sweater from behind her desk.

Hayley craned her neck to see if Sam was in his office

or the examining room. She hoped to heaven he couldn't hear this conversation.

"Why not?" Hayley repeated softly, dumbfounded. "You're the one who told me he hadn't changed. That he would be the town bad boy now and forever. You told me not to lose my heart to him. He's only temporary, you know. He's going to leave. Have you noticed the calendar on his wall? He puts an X through every day that passes. You know he can't wait to leave. He's only here because he owes it to us and to Grandpa."

"Does that mean you can't invite him to dinner now and again? What kind of hostess are you? I heard he eats in the diner every night. That kind of punishment I wouldn't wish on my worst enemy," Mattie said.

"Well then, you invite him to dinner," Hayley said, even more astounded by Mattie's change of attitude than she showed.

"You know he's been treating people for nothing, don't you?"

"He shouldn't do that," Hayley said.

"Only the ones who can't pay. Who've been laid off at the mill or something," Mattie said. "I thought he was a money-grubbing surgeon."

That's what he wants you to think, Hayley thought.

"But he isn't," Mattie continued. "I didn't think he'd really changed. But he has. You could do worse, you know."

Hayley's mouth fell open in surprise. Mattie admitting she'd been wrong about Sam? Mattie suggesting that she and Sam— No, that couldn't be.

There was a loud knock at the front door. Normally patients walked in, so both Hayley and Mattie went to the door and opened it. A small boy stood there holding a half crate of fresh raspberries in his arms. They invited him in, but he shook his head and stayed on the front porch.

"Is the doctor here?" he asked.

"I'll get him," Mattie said, and went back inside. The boy shifted from left to right foot. Hayley stood in the doorway, noting his frayed blue jeans, his faded shirt, feeling almost as awkward as he did, not knowing what to say or do.

When Sam came to the door, the boy held the box out in front of him, but didn't meet Sam's gaze. His ears turned pink with embarrassment. "These are for you. Thanks for patching me up."

Sam bent down to look at his face, placing his hand under the boy's chin. "Looks like you're healing okay."

"My ma is still gonna pay you," the boy said.

Sam raised his eyebrows. "That's not necessary. I told you you didn't have to—" He studied the boy's face for a long moment, then he reached for the box. "Thanks," he said. "They look good."

"Beautiful," Hayley murmured. "Those would make good jam or pie."

The boy nodded, then turned and walked away.

"You wouldn't take his money if he handed it to you, would you, Sam?" Hayley asked.

"I'd rather have the berries. I like it that he picked them himself. It's important for people to pay their way somehow, no matter how poor they are," he explained.

Hayley nodded, remembering how Sam once worked for her grandfather to pay off his debt, unpacking boxes of supplies for him and thumbing through medical books when he thought no one was looking. But Grandpa was looking, and noticing. No wonder Grandpa put him through medical school. It wasn't all charity. It was an investment in the future. An investment in Sam.

Sam handed the box to Hayley, telling her to take them home and do something with them, then he turned to Mattie. "You promised to come and see me when Hayley got here."

"Not today, Sam, I mean Doctor Prentice. I've got too many errands to run."

Sam frowned. "Tomorrow then. No more excuses."

"What's that all about?" Hayley asked when Mattie had picked up her purse and left for the day.

"Sorry. Doctor-patient privilege."

"But...is this about her heart problem?"

He nodded but didn't elaborate, and that was all she got out of him.

That night in the evening, after she'd got caught up on her bills, she made a berry pie. As she rolled out the dough for the crust she thought about Sam. What on earth did Mattie mean, "You could do worse?" As if Sam were hers for the asking. If Mattie only knew what Sam had told her. That he had no intention of marrying anyone, that he was only interested in a short-term affair, for the purpose of "getting her out of his system." That would change Mattie's mind in a second.

But what if it worked? What if a few months of making love with Sam really did cure her of him? Maybe he was right. Because abstinence wasn't working at all. She thought about him day and night. She sneaked glances at him over the breakfast table, watched him walk down the street in the morning from the safety of the living room, memorized the way he walked, talked, even occasionally smiled, tilted his head. And she fantasized about waking up in the morning next to him, pulling the covers over their bodies after a night of lovemaking.

Just as she was arguing with herself over the dubious

merits of his idea, she heard him come through the front door.

The sweet smell of the berry pie drew Sam to the kitchen. That and the promise of a glimpse of Hayley with her cheeks flushed from the heat of the oven. It was taking every bit of his willpower to keep his distance from her. He had suspected but he really hadn't known how hard it was going to be to live and work with her. He racked his brain to think of reasons for staying away from her and her house. The house that reflected her warmth, her love and her generosity. The house that should be filled with a family. Her family. What kind of man had her husband been that he would turn his back on her for a cause? What kind of man wouldn't want to have children with her?

He stood in the kitchen doorway looking at her, imagining what her children would look like, little blond imps with her blue eyes and her stubborn little chin and her determination and willpower. She looked up and smiled at him. His heart lurched in his chest. God, she was beautiful.

"Want some pie?" she asked.

"Sure." He shouldn't stay there in the kitchen. He ought to go upstairs. STAT. Before he said something stupid. Before he did something he'd be sorry for.

"I'll put the coffee on," she said.

He caught her by the arm as she turned to the stove. "Look, Hayley. I'm sorry I pressured you the other night. I had no business. You were right. One night was enough. We don't need six months of making love to know that it's over between us."

She blinked. "Did I say that?"

"Something like that."

She moistened her lips with her tongue, and he felt a rush of desire so strong he rocked back on his heels.

"That's funny," she said with a catch in her voice. "I was thinking I was wrong and you were right."

"You mean you're not over me yet?" he asked incredulously, his heart pounding furiously, his hopes rising like phoenix out of the ashes of disappointment.

She shook her head.

"We could give it one more night, if you think that would help," he suggested as soberly as he could, when he felt as though his chest would burst. She gave a little shrug of her shoulders, which he took to be an affirmative. Then he did it. He claimed her with a kiss. He'd told himself if he ever got another chance, he'd take it slow. But all of his plans suddenly went out the window. The thought that this was something Hayley wanted, that she'd actually, well, almost suggested, made him throw restraint out the window. It was like an aphrodisiac that he didn't really need.

She responded to his kiss with one of her own. Then another and another. His need for her grew by the minute. The more he took, the more he wanted. The more she gave, the more desperate he was for more. Their kisses were deeper, longer, and yet never deep or long enough. He wanted to possess her. But he couldn't. She tasted like the sweetest berries he'd eaten. And he couldn't get enough. He never would.

With his fingers splayed across her back, he drew her close, until she was nestled against his aching erection. She moaned softly, then grabbed his hand, and they raced up the staircase to her room. The room that could only be hers, with the air redolent with the scent of the roses that grew on the trellis beneath her window, the pale, lush carpet, the small old-fashioned fireplace laid with kindling for cool-evening fires, the soft, hand-woven rug in front of it, the bed with its smooth sheets.

He'd dreamed of this room. When he was a teenager he'd imagined her in a pink room with piles of pillows. Like a picture he'd seen in a magazine. With a bulletin board holding the pictures of her friends and dried flowers that her admirers had given her. But she'd grown up. And so had her room. This was not imagination. This was real. Hayley drew the curtains and dimmed the light and, with reckless abandon, tossed her clothes on the white wicker chair at her desk. No more the shy girl he'd once known, she was a woman now, a woman who knew what she wanted. He felt the blood pound in his temples as he realized she wanted him.

He dropped his pants to the floor, then he ripped off his shirt and next his boxers. He felt her heated gaze on his body as they stood facing each other, waiting, wanting, wondering who would make the first move. She was so beautiful he couldn't stop staring at her. He wanted to memorize the way her breasts curved upward, the way her dusky nipples peaked, the mole on her hip, the flush that spread over her pale skin as he stood staring.

Her body called to him like a siren to the ancient mariners, and he knew it was inevitable, this coming together. He'd always known it. Known that somehow, some day this would happen. It would be him and Hayley in her room, in her bed. The first time they'd almost made love was years ago in the playhouse, the first time they'd really made love, only days ago, had been a fluke. This time, this time, he would make it last. He would make it one to remember. Just in case it was the last and there were no more. The tension built, the throbbing in his temple became more intense, and he thought he might pass out before he ever made it to her big, soft bed.

She held out her arms then, and he crushed her to him, unable to wait any longer. He lifted her, and she wrapped

her legs around his waist and threw her arms around his
neck, so her bare breasts nestled against his chest. She was
breathing hard and so was he. He carried her to the bed
as the breeze blew the curtains and the dull roar of the
ocean faded into the distance.

This time it was Hayley who braced herself on the bed
above him, her hands next to his shoulders, her eyes
gleaming. He clenched his jaw, trying to keep his need in
check. Trying to do what he said he would do—go slow.
But he didn't know she was going to take charge.

"Hayley, for God's sake…" he said.

"Relax, Sam," she said, bending over to let her breasts
brush against his chest, her lips trail whisper-soft kisses
along the outline of his jaw.

"Relax?" he groaned. And caught her face between his
broad hands to devour her mouth. No more soft kisses.
These were harsh, demanding kisses, one after another.
Her tongue met his in a dance of recognition, tangled with
his until he was sure he couldn't wait another minute. This
was agony but it was ecstasy, too.

But she wasn't ready for him yet. She broke the kiss
and made a tour of his body with her mouth. She began
at his chest where her tongue stroked one flat nipple, making him feel as if he was floating somewhere above the
bed, having an out-of-body experience. How else to explain this feeling that he was on a different level of pleasure than he'd ever been on before? That he'd never
wanted anyone as much as he wanted Hayley right now.
That if he didn't enter her in the next second he would
very likely explode.

It became clear she had no intention of stopping there.
She wanted him on her terms, and she wanted to take him
into her mouth. Into her hot, wet mouth. He had to make
her stop, and yet he didn't want her to stop. If she did, he

might die, but he would die a happy man. When she finally did stop, he entered her like a turbo charger, thrusting himself inside her at last. Until he was home, where he wanted to be, where he was meant to be. Where he burst into a thousand fragments as he shattered and called her name.

She cried out at the same time and collapsed on top of him.

They lay in her bed, perspiring, coupled together until he rolled over and covered them with her flowered sheet. Her eyes were closed, her hair curled damply on her cheek. His heart swelled. He wanted to take care of her. Though she was perfectly capable of taking care of herself, he had a primeval, male desire to watch over her and keep her safe.

It was a good thing he had six months to get her out of his system, because he wasn't any closer to his goal now than he'd been the day he arrived. Would she ever cease to surprise him? Amaze him? Delight him? Would he ever be able to enjoy another woman again? Did it matter? The answer was no. He'd take whatever Hayley would give and forget about the future. The hell with other women. He would go back to work and forget other women. Maybe he would even forget Hayley. Yeah, sure.

While this impossible thought played havoc with his mind and with Hayley wrapped in his arms, he fell asleep. When he woke in the middle of the night she sighed and rubbed her cheek against his.

"Oh, Sam," she murmured. He was instantly aroused by the smell of her hair, the touch of her skin and the swell of her breasts against his chest. Sleepily, slowly, sweetly, they made love again until he tasted, breathed and smelled nothing but her. He no longer knew where she left off and he began. He felt as though the wall around his heart was crumbling, and as a heart surgeon that was a phenomenon he was sure didn't exist. At least, he'd never encountered it in the literature. But what else would make him feel so vulnerable, so raw inside?

In the morning he was dimly aware she was getting out of bed, going downstairs and baking something as she always did, even though he was the only guest. She was kneading the baking powder biscuits when he came downstairs. He stood in the doorway looking at her, wondering what it would be like if it lasted forever. Until he crushed that thought like an ant under the heel of his shoe.

"Hi," she said, when she sensed his presence and looked up. She gave him a slow, sweet half smile, and desire slammed into him like a redwood tree off a logging truck. What was wrong with him? After a night of lovemaking, he was still not sated.

He stopped on the far side of the room, because if he got close to her he didn't know what he might do. Take her back to bed was one thing that leaped to mind. But he was on his way to work. "I overslept," he said, his voice rusty. "Got an early appointment. See you later." He meant to walk out the door, but something drew him back. That something was Hayley. He got halfway through the living room, came back, lifted her up, felt her arms go around his neck and kissed her. A kiss that said he'd be back. That he wanted more and that she meant something to him.

When Hayley finally caught her breath, she went to the front door and stood in the doorway in her jeans and sweater and apron and watched him go. She pressed her fingers against her lips and tried to understand what was happening. She was falling in love with Sam again, that she knew. But what about him? She knew he'd felt something. She knew he cared about her. And she knew it was more than getting her out of his system. How much more she didn't know. She decided she really didn't want to know.

When the phone rang, she was hanging sheets to dry behind the house for that sunshine-fresh fragrance her guests expected. She took the portable phone from the pocket of her shirt and said, "Bancroft House."

"Ms. Bancroft, this is Charles Ross. I saw your ad for a family practitioner on the bulletin board at my medical school."

Hayley's knees wobbled. Dropping the wet sheet in the grass, she staggered to the bench next to the rose garden. "Are you...did you...?"

"I just passed my boards in family practice and I'm looking for a job in a small town. Is the position still open?"

Hayley's mouth was so dry she could hardly speak. It was the answer to her prayers. Hers and the whole town's. But if this young man came, then Sam would have to go.

"Open? Yes, yes it is. How soon—I mean when can you be available...to come for an interview?"

"Whenever you say. I'm finished with school. I could drive up in a couple of days, be there say, Friday. Would that be convenient?"

"Yes, yes, it would." Hayley gave him directions and invited him to spend the night at her inn, then she hung up. She stared at her mother's rose garden for a long time. She ought to be jumping up and down with glee. She ought to be on the phone to the members of the search committee right now. She told herself she didn't want to get their hopes up, not yet. After all, Charles might change his mind. He might hate it there. He might not be qualified. But deep down she knew he was qualified. And she knew he'd like it there. He sounded so young, so polite, so earnest. So different from Sam.

She didn't tell Sam about the call when she went in to work that afternoon. She didn't tell Mattie, either. There was plenty of time to do that. She had all week. But as the week went by she didn't tell anyone. She suffered guilt pangs every time she looked at Sam. Which was frequently. Which was all the time. She couldn't keep her eyes off him.

Every night that week they made incredible, wonderful love. Hayley managed to keep her worries at bay, her fears and her doubts too. She knew it would end. Even if Charles didn't work out, Sam would leave. The uncertainty gave a frantic edge to her lovemaking that Sam noticed.

"Hey," he said, massaging her bare back as she lay across his bed. "You're tense."

"You've got me working too hard," she said lightly. "Sending lab samples to Portland. Restraining kids while you immunize them. Ohh, that feels good. Do that again."

He shifted his position so he could knead the muscles in her neck. "Sure that's all?" he asked.

"Sure." She didn't know why she couldn't tell him. He was going to find out soon enough. She planned to tell him Thursday night before Charles came.

But that night Mattie called him at home, complaining of chest pains. He told her he'd be right over. "She was moving her furniture around, after I strictly forbade her from any exertion," Sam told Hayley before he walked out the door. "I should have known she wouldn't obey me. She still thinks I'm a kid who doesn't know what he's talking about. If your grandfather had told her—"

"No, she'd still do exactly what she wanted to. That's Mattie. If this is a heart attack, maybe I ought to call an ambulance,'' Hayley said, trying to keep calm while she went to the phone.

"I'll let you know," he said, and grabbed his black bag which looked strangely similar to the one Grandpa used. Which made him look like the GP he said he never wanted to be.

"Should I come?" she asked.

"I'll call you," he repeated, and he was gone.

She paced the floor, she ironed sheets, she started a loaf of bread, though it was ten o'clock. And still he didn't call. She didn't dare call Mattie's house, but she couldn't stand the suspense much longer.

Finally Sam came back at midnight, looking as haggard as if he'd put in a day's work in the OR. "She's going to be okay," he said. "Stubborn old girl. Wasn't taking her medicine."

Hayley gave a sigh of relief and sank into the armchair by the fireplace. "For what? What's wrong with her heart?"

"She's got atherosclerosis. Her arteries are clogged with plaque. This was an angina attack, a warning."

"How is she?"

"Resting comfortably. I gave her some nitroglycerin. And prescribed a significant weight loss. She also needs a good workup. An EKG, blood tests, the whole nine yards. At a hospital, of course. I know a good heart man in Portland she should see."

"Did she agree?"

"She doesn't have a choice. I said either she lets me call an ambulance or I'll put her in the back seat of my car and drive her there myself. That's her choice."

Hayley smiled to herself thinking of Mattie and Sam locking horns over her treatment. She wasn't surprised to hear that Sam won.

"I should call her cousin in Spokane," Hayley said.

"I already did that," Sam said.

"You look tired," she said.

"Treating one stubborn Mattie Whitlock is equal to a day in surgery," he said. "She tried to tell me she was fine. She tried to kick me out. Doesn't want to take her medicine or go to a hospital. Said her mother died in a hospital."

Hayley shook her head. "You'd think after all these years in the office—"

"That's another thing. She quotes your grandfather whenever it suits her. "'Doc Bancroft told me I wasn't overweight. Doc Bancroft told me exertion wouldn't hurt me.' And on and on." A few weeks ago these words of Sam's would have been tinged with bitterness. Now he sounded faintly amused at her devotion to the old doctor.

"I'm sure she gave Grandpa just as hard a time when he was here. That's the way it goes. Now that he's gone, she's promoted him to godly status. You never appreciate anyone until they leave."

"So after I go is when you'll appreciate me?" he asked with a wry smile.

That was the time for her to tell him about Charles Ross. But when she opened her mouth to speak, the words didn't come out. Maybe she didn't want to spoil this night. Maybe she was afraid he'd leave immediately. Maybe she was just plain scared to lose him. Although it wasn't possible to lose something you never had.

So she didn't say anything. She lay in his arms all night trying to get the courage to tell him, but she never did. It felt too good to lie there surrounded by his warmth, his strength and the knowledge that he cared about her. She wasn't willing to give that up. Not yet. She went to work with Sam that morning to fill in for Mattie, and the office was so busy she didn't get a chance to tell him then, either. Not that she tried very hard.

Ten

Sam sent Hayley home for lunch while he wrote up some notes on patients he'd seen that morning after he'd made an early house call on Mattie. There was Mrs. Pritchard with her arthritis, who seemed to be improving with the new drug he'd read about on the Internet. And a little girl with an ear infection he was treating with antibiotics, who'd given him a crayon drawing of herself that he'd tacked on the wall. On the plus side of his coming to New Hope, he had to admit none of his heart patients in San Francisco had ever drawn a picture for him. But on the minus side, he hadn't really saved any lives since he'd been there either. Hadn't given any lectures or had anyone say he'd made a brilliant diagnosis.

The other plus was coming to grips with his ignominious departure from town the last time. He had to admit, now that he was in Doc Bancroft's shoes, that he, too, would report a teenage kid who came to his office with a gunshot wound. For the kid's sake as well as it being the law. He hadn't told Hayley, but he would. She deserved to know he was no longer bitter about that. He was and had always been grateful to the old man for saving his eye after the bullet had grazed his forehead in a fight he hadn't started and wanted no part of.

But he'd also been angry as only an eighteen-year-old punk could be that he'd been blamed for getting shot at. Angry that the doctor had called the police and the police had come looking for him. Sure, he wasn't at fault, but who would have believed him besides Hayley? So he hit the road, determined never to return, determined to make something of himself.

No, he was no longer bitter, no longer angry. Come to think of it, he didn't feel bitter about much these days. He felt a strange sense of what might be called serenity if he didn't know better. He wasn't the serene type. This strange new feeling had something to do with the fact that he'd revisited the Red Barn, gone inside, had a beer and walked out. His father was nowhere to be seen or heard. He was gone. Forever. Not that he would ever forget the lesson he'd learned from him. Deep down he knew now what kind of father he would be. Not that he was planning to be anyone's father, but now he knew. And of course the main reason for his new outlook on life was due to Hayley. She was everything he'd dreamed of and more. She was his first love, or she would have been if he'd been capable of loving at the time. Not that he loved her now. He still didn't know what love was. Wouldn't know if it hit him in the face. It didn't matter. From what he could see it was badly overrated. What counted was trust. And he trusted Hayley. He also thought she was the sexiest woman in the world. Whether she was wearing jeans or a dress or a white smock at the office or best of all—nothing at all. He was glad he would have time to get over her before he left town. He was sure that's what it would take—time. Time and a little effort. But he wasn't quite there yet.

He got up from his office chair when he heard someone in the waiting room. He didn't have any more appointments so it had to be a drop-in. He hoped it wasn't an emergency. In fact it was a healthy-looking young man in a short-sleeved white shirt, gray pants and glasses. He'd never seen him before. But despite attending Rotary meetings with Pete Lamb and hanging out in the diner now and then, he still didn't know everyone in New Hope.

"Is Ms. Bancroft here?" the young man asked, looking around the office.

"Just stepped out for lunch. Can I help you?" Sam asked.

"I...I spoke to her on the phone about the job. She said to go to her house, but I got lost and someone pointed me here."

Lost. The job. Spoke to her on the phone. The words echoed in the small office. Sam knew what they meant, but the meaning still wasn't clear. It couldn't be what he thought it was. She would have told him. "The job?" he repeated as calmly as he could.

"Family practitioner. I saw the ad on the bulletin board. She told me the job was still open."

"When was this?" Sam asked, his lips stiff, feeling as if his blood had been replaced with ice water.

"Sunday, I guess, or was it Monday? I saw the job posted at school, so I called right away. She said to come for an interview and to look around the town." He smiled. "Here I am."

"Here you are," Sam said, gritting his teeth. He couldn't believe she hadn't told him. The woman he trusted. This must be a misunderstanding. "Come on in and sit down," he said. "She should be back soon."

"Are you..." Charles began, after he'd taken a seat in the office across from Sam's desk. Sam realized that all this time he'd thought of the old oak desk with the deep file drawers as Doc Bancroft's...until now. What was he doing, staking his claim? Ridiculous. He didn't want the desk. He didn't want the office. He didn't want the practice.

"I'm Sam Prentice. I'm filling in until they find someone permanent," Sam said. He'd said these words over and over when people asked. They rolled out of his mouth without thinking. But today they took on a new meaning. His time was limited. He could be gone tomorrow. He suddenly realized he didn't want to be gone tomorrow or the next day. Not that he wanted to stay forever or for longer than the six months. But he wasn't ready to leave yet. He had things he wanted to do. Get Mattie into the city for her tests. Find an effective medication for Mr. O'Leary's bursitis. Do the six-week checkup for Shawnee's baby. Remove the cast on the Higgins boy's arm. Get over Hayley. No, he wasn't ready to leave the office yet.

He kept thinking he'd be able to cure himself of his obsession with her. Of his dependence on her smile, the lilt of her voice, the smell of her coffee in the morning. Her calm, quiet presence in the office, her company in the evening when they talked over the cases he'd seen. Making passionate love every night and waking up with her in the morning.

"You're a family practitioner?" the young man asked.

"I'm a surgeon," Sam said brusquely. "My practice is in San Francisco. I'm taking a sabbatical."

Charles glanced around the office. "But—"

"I know, there's no hospital here, no place to do surgery. I've had to do things here I hadn't done since med school. But I'm originally from New Hope, I wanted to come back and help out." What a lie. He'd hated coming back. He'd been forced to come back.

"Looks like a nice town."

"You think so? Have you seen any other small towns?"

"As a matter of fact, this is my fourth interview. All small towns. That's where I want to be," Charles said.

"You must like it quiet. There's no excitement here unless you count the kite festival this summer. The town's in a recession. Have you been on Main Street? Not much traffic, stores closed up. Logging operations cut way back. Commercial fishing down. Not much money to be made here, if that's a consideration."

Charles nodded. "Well, yes, I'd like to get married and buy a house someday."

"That's another thing. All the good women have left town or are already married."

"What about Ms. Bancroft?" Charles asked.

Sam glared at him. The nerve of the guy. Was he suggesting...was he asking— "What about her?" Sam demanded.

"Is she married?"

"She's too old for you," Sam said bluntly.

Charles blushed. Proving that he was much too young for Hayley. Much too inexperienced.

"She sounded young on the phone," Charles said.

"She's my age, thirty-five. But there are other women," he conceded, "and there are houses for sale, some good bargains, due to the exodus."

"Anything with a view of the ocean? I always wanted a house overlooking the water."

"You might be able to find one," Sam said, admitting

to himself that he'd grown attached to the ever-changing view of the sea from his room at the Bancroft House. "But what about professionally? Can you live without colleagues to discuss your cases with, to exchange ideas, to keep you up to date?"

"I plan to attend conferences," Charles said earnestly. "And take classes over the Internet. They have some excellent new CDs available on everything from heart transplants to new treatments for asthma."

"And how to deliver a breech baby," Sam muttered, standing. "But they're no substitute for working in a big hospital with other doctors."

Charles drew his eyebrows together, clearly concerned. As well he should be.

"Come on, I'll show you what we've got here," Sam said. "It isn't much."

Hayley came back from lunch, wondered about the strange car in front of the office, then stood in the waiting room listening to the conversation between the two men. She was frozen to the spot, unable to stride boldly into the office and interrupt them, to deny the town was in a recession, that there was no excitement or stimulation in New Hope. How could she? Everything Sam said was true. But it was possible to put a more positive spin on it. Sam hadn't chosen to do that. Everything he said reflected his negative outlook on New Hope. She thought he'd changed his viewpoint. Obviously he hadn't, which made a wave of sadness sweep over her as high as the tide.

She'd hoped by now Sam might see the good side of life in New Hope, the satisfaction of taking care of the people here. She should have known better. He was only marking time. As for her, she meant nothing to him. A diversion to fill in the empty hours. His remark about all the good women having left town hurt like a needle stuck in her heart.

When the two men strolled out into the waiting room ten minutes later, Charles had just said something like, You must be anxious to get back to your practice, and Sam answered, ''The sooner the better.''

Hayley felt a rush of anger. If he wanted to go so badly, why couldn't he have helped her to find a replacement? Why couldn't he convince this man that he'd be happy here? Careful not to show her anger in front of this prospect, she forced a smile to her face.

''You must be Charles Ross,'' she said, holding out her hand. ''I'm Hayley Bancroft. Sorry I wasn't here to greet you.''

''That's okay. Dr. Prentice has been showing me around.''

''And giving you an earful. Yes, I heard,'' she said. She shifted her gaze to Sam. He shot her a lethal look. He might be just as angry as she was. For different reasons. ''Would you like to come back to the house now?'' she asked the newcomer.

''I thought I'd look around town, if you don't mind,'' he said. ''I've got to think about this.''

''I'll get my car and take you,'' she offered. If she only had a chance to counter Sam's opinions with her own and with others she could introduce him to.

''Please don't bother. I'll hook up with you tonight.''

''Dinner's at seven,'' she said.

He got directions to her house, thanked Sam, and walked down the street with a long stride. So young, so eager, so inexperienced, so impressionable. A few words from a successful, experienced doctor, one whose actual hometown was New Hope had replaced his enthusiasm with doubts. If only she'd been there when he arrived.

They needed him; she wanted him to take the job; he was the answer to her prayers. And yet...and yet...what about Sam?

Hayley stood in the empty waiting room looking out the window, aware of Sam's eyes on her, burning holes in her back. The silence grew along with the tension, until it was thick as the morning fog along the coast. She couldn't stand it another minute. But before she could turn on her heel and face him, he grabbed her arm and spun her around.

"When were you going to tell me someone was coming to take my place?" he demanded, his eyes narrowed, his mouth set in a grim, straight line.

She took a shallow breath. "There's nothing certain. He's just an applicant."

"*Just* an applicant. Your only applicant. You've known for days he was coming. This is important. You didn't answer my question," he said. "When were you going to tell me?"

"Answer this," she said, ignoring his question. "Why did you do your utmost to discourage him?"

"I told him the truth, that's all. There's nothing here," he said flatly.

Hayley felt as though he'd stabbed her in the back. "Nothing" included the practice, the people and especially her. She didn't know what to say next. He'd plunged a knife into her. Now he was twisting it. She was spared from answering when a patient came in the front door. Then another and another. She wanted to leave but she couldn't. She was desperate to get out of his sight. But he needed her to find the patients' charts, to take temperatures and make appointments.

She thought they were working normally together, as smoothly and efficiently as ever, but he complained when she spent too much time talking with a patient, and she was late getting to the examining room with a syringe. Gone was their camaraderie achieved over the past weeks. The tight lines were back around his mouth and furrowed into his forehead. She thought he'd changed, but he hadn't. He looked just the way he did the day he'd arrived. Tense, irritable and testy.

After the last patient left, she paused in the doorway to his office. "Are you coming to dinner?" she asked.

"Is he coming?" Sam asked.

"I assume so," she said coolly.

"Then I'll be there."

"You're afraid I'll brainwash him, aren't you?" she asked.

"I'm afraid you'll seduce him."

Hayley paled. The implication was clear: I'm afraid you'll seduce him...the way you seduced me. Her knees shook, and she felt as though she might faint. She gathered all her strength, took a step forward and slapped him across the face. Stunned, he jerked backward.

"I deserved that," he muttered, rubbing his hand over his cheek.

"Yes, you did." She marched out of the office then, leaving him standing there, his eyes glazed, his cheek still carrying the imprint of her hand. She walked home in a daze, passing a few people on the sidewalk without speaking, without seeing them. She'd never struck anyone in her life. Not in anger, not in frustration. She didn't believe in violence. But she wasn't sorry she'd done it.

He didn't come to dinner. She wasn't surprised. Charles wasn't, either. He said he'd run into Sam in the diner having a cup of coffee after work. Hayley found she had no need to brainwash or seduce Charles into taking the job. Not that she would have done either. He was convinced to give New Hope serious consideration by the time he arrived for cocktails in the living room. Over dessert he said he'd like to hang around for a week and see if it was the right place for him.

"Sam told me I'd like it here," Charles said, balancing his plate of crème caramel on his lap on the couch.

"Sam said that?" she asked. He must have realized that if Charles stayed, he could leave. "It's a wonderful town, but then, I'm prejudiced," Hayley said. "What else did Sam say?"

"He said it was a great place to live and bring up kids. There's really everything a person could want—fresh air, friendly people, fishing…. Honest to God, when he finished talking about the quality of life here, the friends he'd made, the patients he'd treated, I almost felt sorry for him, going back to San Francisco."

"I wouldn't feel too sorry for him," Hayley said dryly. "He has everything he wants there. If I didn't know him so well, I'd say he was giving you a sales talk."

Charles nodded. "Maybe. But I've been through other interviews and I think I know when somebody's being insincere. I think he really believes it. He's an interesting guy. At first I thought he was one of those arrogant, hotshot surgeons who's full of himself. But underneath he's really a good person. I, uh, it's none of my business, and maybe you know it—" Charles's face turned red as he spoke "—but that guy has it bad for you."

Hayley shook her head. Sam had really done a number on Charles. Talked him into spending some time in New Hope while giving the impression that he was interested in her. Which he had been. For a while. Now it was over. Sam could leave with a clear conscience, now that they had a solid prospect. She couldn't help it, she had to ask. "What makes you say that?"

"He said something about you."

Hayley didn't want to hear what he had to say about her. But she was a glutton for punishment. "Go on."

"He said you were everything that was good about New Hope. You're honest and kind and generous, unpretentious." Charles pushed his glasses up his nose and looked at her through his thick lenses. "The man acts as though he's in love with you and with the town. But if he is, then why…? I don't get it. Well, anyway, I'm keeping my options open."

Hayley opened her mouth to beg him to accept the job, to forget his other options, because Sam was going and going for good, but instead of speaking she set her coffee cup down abruptly and went to the kitchen. She stood there, gripping the edge of the counter while the tears streamed down her face. She knew that whatever happened, Sam would leave as soon as he could and he'd never be back. She knew, too, that all hopes of forgetting him were futile. She would never be able to walk into his room without remembering the night she'd first made love with him.

Damn him. Damn him for saying something nice about her, damn him for making her indebted to him for convincing Charles to stay, for spoiling her for anyone else, for making it impossible for her to live in her own house without being haunted by his presence…without seeing him every time she went to the kitchen, to the garden or slept in her bedroom.

Of course she got over it. She stopped crying in a few hours. In the morning, after a sleepless night spent listening for Sam's car, a bleary-eyed Hayley was suffering a monumental headache. At the office, she found Sam had written a detailed history of every patient for Charles, what treatment he recommended and a little character sketch.

He must have been up all night working on it, then he'd left town quietly without leaving so much as a note for her or picking up his things at the house. He was that anxious to avoid her. She didn't care. She would ship them to him. But she couldn't stand to even pack them up. Not yet.

As the days passed, every time she went into the room he'd occupied, she was hit with the faint smell of his shaving lotion and the memories of their nights together. She couldn't believe he would walk out on her like that. Couldn't believe he didn't think of her from time to time. Believe it, she told herself. She meant nothing to him. It was time to get that through her head.

It was especially hard to get it through her head when she talked to Mattie at her house where she was recovering.

"I can't leave the office for a week without everything falling apart," Mattie complained, wearing a velour robe and sitting across from Hayley at Mattie's pine kitchen table.

"Nothing has fallen apart," Hayley assured her. "There has been a seamless transition. Wait till you meet Charles."

"Already met him. Awfully young, isn't he? Yes, he came to see me as soon as I got back from Portland. Said Sam told him to. Said I can go back to work next week. I asked him if he's staying for good. Told him Doc Bancroft was in practice for sixty years. He said he couldn't promise anything. Said he wouldn't leave until we had a replacement. What's that mean?" Mattie didn't wait for an answer. "When I get back you can take some time off. You look terrible."

Hayley smiled weakly. "Thank you, Mattie." She stood up to refill her teacup, afraid Mattie would see beyond her pale face and the dark smudges under the eyes into her broken heart.

"What's wrong with Sam, taking off like that?" Mattie asked.

"Nothing. Charles came, so we don't need him anymore," Hayley said, not mentioning that Charles hadn't signed a contract, preferring to wait until he was sure this was the right place for him. She intended to make an effort to convince him as soon as she could. But right now she didn't seem to have the energy to convince anybody of anything. Least of all to convince herself that she wasn't in love with Sam

"Humph. Told you, you should have invited him to dinner more often."

"His leaving had nothing to do with me," Hayley said.

"You expect me to believe that?" Mattie asked. "After I saw the way he looked at you, the way you looked at him. I may have a bad heart, but my eyes are working just fine. Something was going on with you two."

"Yes, all right," Hayley admitted with a sigh. "Something was going on, something that we started back in high school. But we're grown up now and it's over. Life goes on."

"How's life going on with Sam?"

"I have no idea," Hayley said.

"Why don't you give him a call or better yet go down and see him."

"I can't do that," Hayley said indignantly. "Even if I wanted to, which I don't, I don't know where he is. He's not supposed to go back to work for another few months."

"He's at home in San Francisco," Mattie said. "He called me this morning to see how I was."

Hayley's mouth fell open in surprise. "How...how thoughtful." She wanted desperately to ask if he'd asked about her, but she pressed her lips together to keep from saying anything.

"He asked about you," Mattie said, and Hayley's heart skipped a beat. She told herself he was just being polite. If he really wanted to know how she was, he could call and ask her himself.

"I suppose he thinks I'm just pining away for him," Hayley said. "I hope you told him I was doing fine," Hayley said.

"Of course," Mattie said. "He's trying to decide what to do with himself. He's considering several options."

Hayley had to bite her lip to keep from asking what they were. "Well," she said. "I'd better be getting back to work. Charles isn't quite sure where everything is."

True to her word, Mattie came back to work full-time, and Hayley had nothing to do. Except for the occasional guests, she felt cast adrift without a purpose to her life. The town still held a certain charm, a new store had opened up on Main Street; she was roundly congratulated for finding a new doctor; the beaches were beautiful; but something was missing. That something was Sam. Her life stretched ahead of her like a long, flat beach leading nowhere.

She picked up the phone a dozen times to call him, but she only got a recorded message from his starchy secretary, saying he was away from his office and if this was an emergency she could "press one." She could call him at home, but she didn't want to ask Mattie for his number and give her the satisfaction of knowing she was trying to reach him.

But Mattie was one jump ahead of her. On the day Charles signed a lease on Grandpa's office, she came by the Bancroft House and handed Hayley Sam's home phone number and address. "Sam's leaving on a trip. Wouldn't you think he needs the clothes he left behind? Seems to me it's a good excuse to take a run down there, bring them to him.''

"Why should I?"

"Because you can't get on with your life until you close this chapter," Mattie said wisely.

"Sam seems to have gotten on with his without closing this chapter.''

"I'm not too sure about that," Mattie said. Before Hayley could ask what on earth she meant by that, Mattie was walking down the walkway to her car. She waved over her shoulder and left Hayley standing in the doorway with the paper clenched in her hand. Burning a hole in her hand. Until she knew she had to do something about it. Mattie was right. It was time for closure.

She packed Sam's belongings into his suitcase and placed it next to hers in the trunk of her grandfather's old car. She drove straight through down Highway 5 to the San Francisco address on the paper Mattie had given her. It was a tall building, a luxury condominium in a posh neighborhood. Hayley ran a comb through her hair, straightened her jacket and squared her shoulders. But she couldn't still her pounding heart. What if he'd left already? What if he slammed the door in her face, which she deserved after slapping him. She almost hoped he would, because if he let her in, she had no idea what she was going to say.

She stood outside the glass doors so long the doorman was giving her a suspicious look. She gave him a brief smile, then went up to the twenty-third floor and knocked on the door.

"Come on in," he yelled. "It's not locked."

She opened the door to a sparsely furnished, high-ceilinged apartment and stood in the middle of the living room on a polished-oak floor, looking out at a spectacular view of the Golden Gate Bridge.

"You're late." Sam's voice came from another room.

Hayley tried to answer, to say she wasn't late and she wasn't who he thought she was, but her throat was too dry.

When she heard Sam's footsteps coming down the long hall, she turned slowly from the window expecting him be so surprised to see her he would gasp or his mouth would drop open in amazement. Instead he stood there looking at her for a long moment, his gaze steady and unwavering.

"It's about time," he said, his voice rusty, as if he'd been saving his voice for a long time.

"You knew I was coming?" she asked.

"Sooner or later," he said. "I've left the door unlocked for the past two weeks."

"Of all the nerve. You are the most arrogant, conceited, self-absorbed—"

He cut her off then by moving toward her, so big, so tall, so sure of himself that she clenched her hands into fists to keep from being overwhelmed by him. He dragged her into his arms, holding her tightly against his hard body. She could smell the warmth from his skin, feel his heart pounding. She didn't fight him. She couldn't. She was one thousand miles from New Hope, but in his arms, she was home.

Her fists relaxed and she sagged against him, wrapped her arms around him and hung on for dear life. Yes, he was everything she said he was, but despite it all, no matter what he was, God help her, she loved him. And if he wouldn't live in New Hope, she'd have to live here. Because life without him was no life at all.

"You're right," he murmured, his breath warm in her ear. "I'm all of the above. But I'm working on it. I'm trying to change. But I need your help. I love you, Hayley,

I've been in love with you for half my life, and I need your love, too.''

"You've got it," she whispered.

"And I need some time. And a change of scene."

She lifted her head and looked into his dark eyes. "How big a change?" she asked.

"Very big. All the way to Africa. You've never been on safari. I've never visited my patient, and I want to see your village."

"Africa!" She choked on a laugh. She was giddy, light-headed and almost hysterical. Did he say Africa? "How can you...how can we..."

He smiled and her heart contracted. If she hadn't been clinging to him she would have fallen down.

"We fly to London," he said. "Spend a few days shopping, sight-seeing, then fly into Nairobi. Hire a Land Rover and a driver—"

She pressed her fingers against his lips. "I get the picture. What then?"

"Then we go to Mombassa..."

"I mean when we come back."

"That's up to you."

"I want to get married," she said firmly.

"Big surprise," he said. "I suppose you want kids, too."

She nodded, her throat suddenly clogged with tears of happiness. Sam and kids and heaven, too. "Yes, oh yes, but I don't know...I might not be able to...I'm not sure—"

"I am," he said firmly, one hand catching her chin so he could look into her eyes and send positive thoughts directly from his soul to hers. "I'm sure that you and I will have a whole houseful of kids. If, that is, we get started right away."

She nodded. If he believed, then so did she. "Where will we live?" she asked, her voice a bare whisper.

"I always wanted to raise my kids in a small town," he said.

She felt like laughing. She felt like crying. She felt as if her heart was overflowing. Without another word, Sam lifted her into his arms and carried her into the bedroom. The waves hit the shore at Fort Point; the gulls swooped over the water, and inside the twenty-third floor of the condominium, Sam took a four-carat diamond ring from a case on his bureau, got down on his knees and asked Hayley to marry him.

Her smile was more dazzling than the morning sun outside. She didn't have to answer. Her kiss said it all.

Epilogue

Old-timers still called it the Bancroft House, though anyone who had come to New Hope within the past seven years called it the Bancroft-Prentice place, the place where the three Prentice kids played kick ball with their friends, built a tree house with their father, splashed in a wading pool on summer days with their mother and took over the playhouse.

Their father, once a heart surgeon, now did research into atherosclerosis in an office he built on the grounds, and commuted once a month to Portland where he gave a seminar at the medical school there. No matter how busy he was, he always made time for surf fishing with his six-year-old son, Matt. And their mother, once a bed and breakfast proprietor, now was a full-time wife and mother.

"You know you're even more beautiful than you were at eighteen," Sam told her one glorious summer day, coming up behind her on the wide verandah and wrapping his arms around her.

"That's because I got everything I ever wanted," she said, leaning back against him. "What about you? I dragged you back here to live. Are you ever sorry?"

"Sorry? Sorry I left that mausoleum I lived in? That job that was leading me to an early grave? You know the answer to that."

"I don't mind hearing it again."

"Okay, here goes," he said, lifting her hair off her nape to brush his lips across her soft skin. "You saved me from a life of loneliness. You taught me to love and trust and to give. You made all my dreams come true—a house, a family, a wife. The most gorgeous, sexiest—"

She turned in his arms. "Okay," she murmured, blushing as if she were seventeen again. "That's enough."

"Wait, there's more," he said. But she cut him off with a kiss. Sam was no more resistible now than he'd been when she first met him or when she married him. For a man who'd never known love, he had found an amazing capacity for giving and receiving it. From the community, from his children and from her.

He lifted her off her feet and spun her around, and in the distance the laughter of their children echoed across the sprawling grounds, reminding them both to always follow your heart, because the heart has its reasons....

* * * * *

Don't miss talented author Carol Grace's next heartwarming love story,

FAMILY TREE,

on sale July 2000 from Harlequin American Romance.

January 2000
HER FOREVER MAN
#1267 by Leanne Banks
Lone Star Families: The Logans

February 2000
A BRIDE FOR JACKSON POWERS
#1273 by Dixie Browning
The Passionate Powers

March 2000
A COWBOY'S SECRET
#1279 by Anne McAllister
Code of the West

April 2000
LAST DANCE
#1285 by Cait London
Freedom Valley

May 2000
DR. IRRESISTIBLE
#1291 by Elizabeth Bevarly
From Here to Maternity

June 2000
TOUGH TO TAME
#1297 by Jackie Merritt

MAN OF THE MONTH

For twenty years Silhouette has been giving you
the ultimate in romantic reads. Come join the
celebration as some of your favorite authors
help celebrate our anniversary with the most
sensual, emotional love stories ever!

Available at your favorite retail outlet.

Where love comes alive™

is proud to present

the **baby** Bank

Where love is measured in pounds and ounces!

A trip to the fertility clinic leads four women to the family of their dreams!

THE PREGNANT VIRGIN (SD#1283)
Anne Eames **March 2000**

HER BABY'S FATHER (SD#1289)
Katherine Garbera **April 2000**

THE BABY BONUS (SD#1295)
Metsy Hingle **May 2000**

THE BABY GIFT (SD#1301)
Susan Crosby **June 2000**

Available at your favorite retail outlet.

Where love comes alive™

SILHOUETTE'S 20TH ANNIVERSARY CONTEST
OFFICIAL RULES
NO PURCHASE NECESSARY TO ENTER

1. To enter, follow directions published in the offer to which you are responding. Contest begins 1/1/00 and ends on 8/24/00 (the "Promotion Period"). Method of entry may vary. Mailed entries must be postmarked by 8/24/00, and received by 8/31/00.

2. During the Promotion Period, the Contest may be presented via the Internet. Entry via the Internet may be restricted to residents of certain geographic areas that are disclosed on the Web site. To enter via the Internet, if you are a resident of a geographic area in which Internet entry is permissible, follow the directions displayed on-line, including typing your essay of 100 words or fewer telling us "Where In The World Your Love Will Come Alive." On-line entries must be received by 11:59 p.m. Eastern Standard time on 8/24/00. Limit one e-mail entry per person, household and e-mail address per day, per presentation. If you are a resident of a geographic area in which entry via the Internet is permissible, you may, in lieu of submitting an entry on-line, enter by mail, by hand-printing your name, address, telephone number and contest number/name on an 8"x 11" plain piece of paper and telling us in 100 words or fewer "Where In The World Your Love Will Come Alive," and mailing via first-class mail to: Silhouette 20th Anniversary Contest, (in the U.S.) P.O. Box 9069, Buffalo, NY 14269-9069; (In Canada) P.O. Box 637, Fort Erie, Ontario, Canada L2A 5X3. Limit one 8"x 11" mailed entry per person, household and e-mail address per day. On-line and/or 8"x 11" mailed entries received from persons residing in geographic areas in which Internet entry is not permissible will be disqualified. No liability is assumed for lost, late, incomplete, inaccurate, nondelivered or misdirected mail, or misdirected e-mail, for technical, hardware or software failures of any kind, lost or unavailable network connection, or failed, incomplete, garbled or delayed computer transmission or any human error which may occur in the receipt or processing of the entries in the contest.

3. Essays will be judged by a panel of members of the Silhouette editorial and marketing staff based on the following criteria:

> Sincerity (believability, credibility)—50%
> Originality (freshness, creativity)—30%
> Aptness (appropriateness to contest ideas)—20%

Purchase or acceptance of a product offer does not improve your chances of winning. In the event of a tie, duplicate prizes will be awarded.

4. All entries become the property of Harlequin Enterprises Ltd., and will not be returned. Winner will be determined no later than 10/31/00 and will be notified by mail. Grand Prize winner will be required to sign and return Affidavit of Eligibility within 15 days of receipt of notification. Noncompliance within the time period may result in disqualification and an alternative winner may be selected. All municipal, provincial, federal, state and local laws and regulations apply. Contest open only to residents of the U.S. and Canada who are 18 years of age or older, and is void wherever prohibited by law. Internet entry is restricted solely to residents of those geographical areas in which Internet entry is permissible. Employees of Torstar Corp., their affiliates, agents and members of their immediate families are not eligible. Taxes on the prizes are the sole responsibility of winners. Entry and acceptance of any prize offered constitutes permission to use winner's name, photograph or other likeness for the purposes of advertising, trade and promotion on behalf of Torstar Corp. without further compensation to the winner, unless prohibited by law. Torstar Corp and D.L. Blair, Inc., their parents, affiliates and subsidiaries, are not responsible for errors in printing or electronic presentation of contest or entries. In the event of printing or other errors which may result in unintended prize values or duplication of prizes, all affected contest materials or entries shall be null and void. If for any reason the Internet portion of the contest is not capable of running as planned, including infection by computer virus, bugs, tampering, unauthorized intervention, fraud, technical failures, or any other causes beyond the control of Torstar Corp. which corrupt or affect the administration, secrecy, fairness, integrity or proper conduct of the contest, Torstar Corp. reserves the right, at its sole discretion, to disqualify any individual who tampers with the entry process and to cancel, terminate, modify or suspend the contest or the Internet portion thereof. In the event of a dispute regarding an on-line entry, the entry will be deemed submitted by the authorized holder of the e-mail account submitted at the time of entry. Authorized account holder is defined as the natural person who is assigned to an e-mail address by an Internet access provider, on-line service provider or other organization that is responsible for arranging e-mail address for the domain associated with the submitted e-mail address.

5. Prizes: Grand Prize—a $10,000 vacation to anywhere in the world. Travelers (at least one must be 18 years of age or older) or parent or guardian if one traveler is a minor, must sign and return a Release of Liability prior to departure. Travel must be completed by December 31, 2001, and is subject to space and accommodations availability. Two hundred (200) Second Prizes—a two-book illustrated edition autographed collector set from one of the Silhouette Anniversary authors: Nora Roberts, Diana Palmer, Linda Howard or Annette Broadrick (value $10.00 each set). All prizes are valued in U.S. dollars.

6. For a list of winners (available after 10/31/00), send a self-addressed, stamped envelope to: Harlequin Silhouette 20th Anniversary Winners, P.O. Box 4200, Blair, NE 68009-4200.

Contest sponsored by Torstar Corp., P.O. Box 9042, Buffalo, NY 14269-9042.

ENTER FOR A CHANCE TO WIN*

Silhouette's 20ᵗʰ Anniversary Contest

Tell Us Where in the World You Would Like *Your* Love To Come Alive... And We'll Send the Lucky Winner There!

Silhouette wants to take you wherever your happy ending can come true.

Here's how to enter: Tell us, in 100 words or less, where you want to go to make your love come alive!

In addition to the grand prize, there will be 200 runner-up prizes, collector's-edition book sets autographed by one of the Silhouette anniversary authors: **Nora Roberts, Diana Palmer, Linda Howard** or **Annette Broadrick**.

DON'T MISS YOUR CHANCE TO WIN! ENTER NOW! No Purchase Necessary

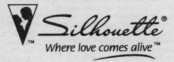

Where love comes alive™

Name:

Address:

City: State/Province:

Zip/Postal Code:

Mail to Harlequin Books: **In the U.S.**: P.O. Box 9069, Buffalo, NY 14269-9069; **In Canada**: P.O. Box 637, Fort Erie, Ontario, L4A 5X3